FREEPORT PUBLIC LIBRARY
100 E. Douglas
Freeport, IL 610
JAN 1 4 2016

D0056373

16
04

Miss Dreamsville and the Lost Heiress of Collier County

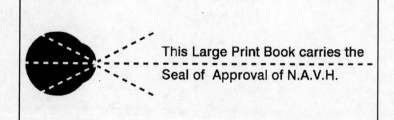

This Large Print Book carries the
Seal of Approval of N.A.V.H.

MISS DREAMSVILLE AND THE LOST HEIRESS OF COLLIER COUNTY

AMY HILL HEARTH

THORNDIKE PRESS
A part of Gale, Cengage Learning

GALE
CENGAGE Learning·

Farmington Hills, Mich • San Francisco • New York • Waterville, Maine
Meriden, Conn • Mason, Ohio • Chicago

GALE
CENGAGE Learning

Copyright © 2015 by Amy Hill Hearth.
Thorndike Press, a part of Gale, Cengage Learning.

ALL RIGHTS RESERVED
This book is a work of fiction. Any references to historical events, real people, or real places are used fictitiously. Other names, characters, places, and events are products of the author's imagination, and any resemblance to actual events or places or persons, living or dead, is entirely coincidental.
Thorndike Press® Large Print Basic.
The text of this Large Print edition is unabridged.
Other aspects of the book may vary from the original edition.
Set in 16 pt. Plantin.

LIBRARY OF CONGRESS CATALOGING-IN-PUBLICATION DATA

Hearth, Amy Hill, 1958–
    Miss Dreamsville and the lost heiress of Collier County / by Amy Hill Hearth. — Large print edition.
        pages cm. — (Thorndike Press large print basic)
    ISBN 978-1-4104-8470-3 (hardcover) — ISBN 1-4104-8470-X (hardcover)
    1. Life change events—Fiction. 2. Literature—Societies, etc.—Fiction. 3. Florida—Intellectual life—Fiction. 4. Large type books. I. Title.
PS3608.E274M58 2016
813'.6—dc23   2015034947

Published in 2016 by arrangement with Atria Books, an imprint of Simon & Schuster, Inc.

Printed in Mexico
1 2 3 4 5 6 7 19 18 17 16

In loving memory of my niece,
Anna Katherine Hill
(1980–2012)

ONE

Dolores Simpson was a woman with a past. Now, depending on your age and where you're from, you might interpret that in a number of ways. Let me assure you, however, that in the southern part of the United States of America, in a certain era, this could mean only one thing: *man trouble.*

This affliction spares few women. Even maiden ladies and great aunties — the ones who smile and nod on the porch, contentedly snappin' peas — have stories of youthful turmoil and shattered dreams.

Dolores Simpson, unfortunately, had what my mama used to call *serious* man trouble. After leading a questionable life in Tampa, Dolores came back home one summer day in 1939 with all her worldly goods in a satchel under one arm and a brandnew baby boy in the other.

Yes, indeed. Serious man trouble.

Home, for Dolores, was one hundred and

twenty miles south of Tampa in God's forgotten paradise, Collier County, which is bordered by the Gulf of Mexico on one side and the edge of the Great Everglades Swamp on the other. In those days, Radio Havana in Cuba was the only station that could be heard on the wireless and alligators outnumbered people by at least ten thousand to one.

Dolores's destination was an abandoned fishing shack that once belonged to her grandfather. The shack sat on stilts on a tidal river which was so wild and forbidding that no one with an ounce of sense would try to live there. Still, it was all Dolores knew. She had failed at city life. She had failed at pretty much everything. The river was a place where she could protect her secrets and nurse her frustration with the world.

And there she stayed, alone except for the son she raised, for twenty-five years.

I, too, hailed from Collier County, but instead of the river or swamps I was raised nearby in Naples, an itty-bitty town with a sandy strip of beach on the Gulf.

I barely knew Dolores Simpson. She was, shall we say, reclusive to an extreme. My only knowledge of her was that she had once been a stripper but now hunted alligators for a living. If she had been a man she would have been admired as a fearless frontiersman.

I wouldn't have known even this much, nor would I have met her, if not for her son, Robbie-Lee. In the late summer of 1962, he and I became friends when we joined a new book club called the Collier County Women's Literary Society. To its members, the club provided a sanctuary of sorts. Each of us was a misfit or outcast in town — in my case, because I had come back home after a divorce — but in the book club we discovered a place to belong.

It is one of the ironies of life that being part of a group can, in turn, lead you to find strength and independence as an individual. That's exactly what happened to Robbie-Lee and me. After a year in the book club, we decided it was time to follow our dreams.

For Robbie-Lee, who loved the theater, the only place on his mind was New York City. He spoke endlessly of Broadway and was determined to get a job there, even if it meant sweeping sidewalks. Dolores, whose maternal instincts kicked in with a mighty roar at the idea of him leaving Collier County, objected to his planned departure, but lost the battle. Robbie-Lee caught a northbound bus on a steamy August morning in 1963.

At the same time Robbie-Lee went north I set off for Mississippi. I was hoping to learn more about my mother, who was born and raised in Jackson. Mama had died without telling me certain things. She never talked about her family, or how she met Daddy, or when and where they got married. All I know is they got hitched at a Methodist church because Mama insisted on having a bona fide preacher conduct the ceremony. They left Mississippi and came to Florida because Naples was Daddy's hometown.

What I hoped to find was kinfolk. An aunt or uncle, perhaps. Or maybe a cousin. Since I was a small child, Mama and I had been on our own. It's painful to say, but Daddy up and left us. At least I hoped to find out why my name is Eudora Welty Witherspoon — "Dora" for short. I could only guess that Eudora Welty, the famed Mississippi writer, had been a friend of Mama's when she was growing up.

As I said, Mama never told me certain things.

I figured I'd go to Jackson for a few weeks or at most several months, but before I knew it I'd been away from Florida for a year. I had made more progress finding out about Mama and her people than I ever could have imagined. All I needed was a little more time to wrap things up and settle them properly. I had a job shelving books at the Jackson Library and I rented a small room in the home of a widow named Mrs. Sheba Conroy. I planned on giving proper notice — I didn't want to leave anyone in the lurch — then head home to Naples.

And then the telegram came.

Two

Poor Mrs. Conroy, my landlady in Jackson. I can still picture her face when she saw the Western Union man through the glass panel of her front door. Even under the best of circumstances Mrs. Conroy was nervous as a rat terrier, and with the arrival of a telegram she was likely to need her fainting couch.

To her generation, a telegram was how they usually found out somebody had died, and even though the modern era had arrived and you could make a long-distance telephone call — especially to a city as large as Jackson — plenty of folks still relied on the Western Union man to deliver urgent news.

I couldn't believe it was for me. I'd never gotten a Western Union in my life and had hoped I never would. For a moment I was tempted to tear it up, unread, and toss it out the window right into Mrs. Conroy's

Gulf Pride azalea bushes. But sooner or later, I knew I'd be outside on my hands and knees searching for the pieces and trying to put them back together. I'd have to know what it said.

Mrs. Conroy was so worked up I thought she was on the verge of an apoplectic fit. She was quivering like Aunt Pittypat in *Gone with the Wind* when the Yankees were shelling Atlanta. "Well?" she shrieked, even before I could read it. "What does it *say*?"

I didn't answer at first. Finally, with my voice all aquiver, I blurted out, "It's bad news."

"I knew it!" Mrs. Conroy wailed. "Somebody died! Oh, Lord! Sweet Jesus . . ."

"Well, I don't know about that," I said, trying to calm us both down. "It just says *something's wrong.* But it doesn't say what."

"Let me see that," she said, yanking it from my hands. " 'Big trouble. Come home now.' " She read the words aloud then looked at me. "What does that mean?"

"I don't know," I said.

"Oh, Lordy, Lordy." Poor Mrs. Conroy was wringing her hands. I'd never actually seen anyone do that, but sure enough, that's what she was doing.

"Mrs. Conroy," I tried to sound respectful, but firm. "Could you leave me alone for a moment so I can think? Just for a moment, please?"

She left reluctantly. I heard her moving pots and pans around in the kitchen. Then she began singing "The Old Rugged Cross," which is a nice old hymn but not great background music when you're trying to figure out who sent a Western Union that upended your life and why.

The sender was none other than the stripper turned alligator-hunter herself, Dolores Simpson.

A horrible thought occurred to me: Maybe something had happened to her son, my friend Robbie-Lee. But he was still in New York City and had just written to me that he was well and happy.

One thing was for sure. Whatever was going on was very serious. If there was ever a woman who didn't rattle easy, it would be Dolores. If she said there was trouble, you can bet grandpa's pet buzzard it was the Gospel truth.

But what kind of trouble? *Whose* trouble?

All of a sudden I wanted to go home. I *had* to go home. And I hated myself for staying away for a whole year, even though it had been a good year and I'd found out some things about Mama and her family that had turned my way of thinking upside down. But I had been fooling myself to think that nothing would change in Naples and that I could go back anytime I wanted and everything would be just as it was.

Most likely, someone had died, just as Mrs. Conroy feared. Since my social life had revolved around my book club, I went over the list of members in my head. Besides Robbie-Lee there was Jackie Hart, who had started the book club and was in good health as far as I knew. Jane Wisniewski, known to all as "Plain Jane," was a poet who made a living writing sexy stories for women's magazines under the name Jocelyn Winston. She was in her late fifties and had never mentioned any health concerns. Priscilla Harmon, who at nineteen was the youngest member of our book club, was at Bethune-Cookman College in Daytona Beach. Miss Lansbury, the librarian who helped us choose our book selections and kept the library trustees from interfering, had gone off to live with her kinfolk, a tribe of local Indians. And then there was Mrs. Bailey White, who, come to think of it, was quite elderly. Ten years older than God, as Mama would have said. But why wouldn't Dolores just say that in the telegram? "So-and-so died. Come home."

Instead, it said "big trouble."

15

Which led me back to Jackie. She'd been a newcomer to Naples, having moved from Boston, of all places, when her husband was hired to work for one of our wealthiest residents, Mr. Toomb. Jackie was glamorous and witty but she had a special talent for upsetting the status quo. If they'd been able to get away with it, the town fathers would have had her tarred and feathered and shipped back north.

The book club upended the grapefruit cart, but that wasn't all. Jackie had also started a secret radio show she called *Miss Dreamsville* on WNOG, "Wonderful Naples on the Gulf." This was the first late-night radio show in Naples. I don't know what goes on in Boston, but in Collier County, Florida, a middle-aged wife and mother like Jackie had no business having her own radio show, especially if it involved the deliberate cultivation of a secret, seductive persona (or to use Jackie's favorite term, "temptress").

Then, Jackie came up with her wildest idea yet. She volunteered to take care of a baby so that its unmarried mother — our book club member, Priscilla — could go to college. Plain Jane and Mrs. Bailey White agreed to help. Now this was an extraordinary offer that would have been considered an act of great Christian charity except for

16

one thing. Priscilla and her baby were colored.

Oh, that was more than enough to cause "big trouble."

And yet it didn't make sense that Dolores Simpson would send the telegram. She held a grudge against Jackie. Why would she care if Jackie was in trouble up to her ears?

Mrs. Conroy had moved on to another hymn, "Up from the Ground He Arose," never my favorite, but at the moment, hearing it sung by Mrs. Conroy with her machine-gun vibrato, made me want to beg for mercy. Although I could have borrowed Mrs. Conroy's telephone I slipped out the front door and scurried to the phone box on the corner. I thought I'd try to call Jackie since Dolores didn't have electricity let alone a phone. As luck would have it, the long-distance operator could not get through to anyone in Collier County. A storm had knocked down the lines in Lee County, north of Collier, and it would be another day or two before calls could go through.

So this is what I did: I borrowed money from Mrs. Conroy. And I took one Trailways bus after another all the way back to Collier County. It was the same route I'd taken a year earlier, only in reverse.

The last stretch from Tampa to Naples on the Tamiami Trail was the longest, or so it seemed. I asked the driver to drop me off at a little side road that led to an area known as Gun Rack Village. It was a sorry excuse for a road, but the only way to get to Dolores Simpson's fishing shack unless you had a small boat with a shallow draft.

The bus driver made me promise to be careful. His warning that I better watch out for swamp things was good advice. I whistled and sang, or banged my hand on my little suitcase, just to keep from catching any snakes or gators by surprise.

I found Dolores sitting on the step to the rickety dock that led to her two-room fishing shack. She was whittling a stick into a small weapon known as a "gig." At any other time and place I would have been wary of someone crafting a spear, but seeing her there, knife in hand, made me feel downright nostalgic. I realized I'd been gone too long. This was the Everglades, the River of Grass. To the Seminole Indians, it was "Pa-hay-okee."

To me, it was simply home.

THREE

Dolores spat out a big stream of tobacco juice. "Well, it's about time you got here," she barked, barely glancing up from her handiwork.

This was not the greeting I expected. "I left as soon as I could," I said, thinking that the least she could do was be impressed, maybe even grateful, that I'd done what she'd asked. "You know, Jackson, Mississippi, is a long way from here. I had to borrow money —"

"I don't care about that," Dolores said.

"Well, are you going to tell me what this is about?" My voice was high and squeaky. I hated that, especially when I was trying to sound confident and mature.

She kept whittling.

"Look, Dolores, I think you owe me an explanation."

She still didn't answer.

"Is this about Jackie Hart from the

book club?"

"That woman's a damn fool, and so is old Mrs. Bailey White and that other gal — what's her name, Plain Jane — who are helping raise that baby."

I had a terrible thought. "Is Priscilla's baby all right?"

"Baby's fine," Dolores said.

"Then what is it?" I must have been on my last good nerve because I spoke sharply. "You sent me a Western Union! What in tarnation is the 'big trouble' you were talking about?"

She finally stopped whittling and looked me eyeball to eyeball.

"Your ex-husband," she said.

"Darryl?"

"Well, that is his name, isn't it?"

I felt my face flush. "I'm surprised, is all." Darryl was a pain in the hindquarters, to be sure, but I would never have put him in the category of "big trouble."

"Well, let me be the first to tell you," Dolores said. "He wants to build houses on my land. And a shopping center! And maybe even a golf course! He's going to fill in this whole stretch of the river and run us all out of here." She dropped her head and took a sharp breath. Maybe, I realized, to cover up a sob.

20

I felt light-headed. "Darryl doesn't have that kind of money," I said finally. "Besides, he's dumb as a post. He doesn't have the smarts to dream up a project like that, or make it happen."

Dolores scoffed so loud she startled a night heron nesting halfway up a tree about thirty feet away.

"Aw, shucks," Dolores called over to the heron, "I ain't going to hurt you. Now just settle down on yer ol' eggs and stop your frettin'."

I looked over toward the mama night heron, my eyes searching until I saw the familiar shape of its beak and the markings on its little head. They were odd-looking birds on account of their yellow eyes with red irises. Plus, they didn't sing. Instead, they made a sound like the cranky old crows that used to raid Mama's sunflower garden the minute we turned our backs.

"Your Darryl has got hisself help — people from up north will be paying for it."

"He's not 'my' Darryl."

"You were married to the idiot for a few years. I thought you could try to talk some sense into him. Besides, who loves this here river more than you do?"

Well, that was true. I was known for bring- ing all kinds of swamp and river critters home with me, which Mama, amazingly, tolerated. After a while, folks around the county had gotten to recognize I had a special talent with turtles. After I rescued an Everglades snapping turtle the size of a truck tire from the middle of U.S. 41, folks started calling me the Turtle Lady. From then on, people brought turtles to me that needed help. Three of them stayed on as pets — Norma Jean, Myrtle, and Castro.

I looked again at the mama heron. A heron nest was a messy-looking pile of sticks, and I remembered, with a flush of shame, that years before I had made fun of one when I'd been out for a walk with Mama in these very swamps. She'd said to me, "Now, it may not look like much to you but no doubt it is perfectly suited to the heron. The heron knows what it's doing, rest assured."

Dolores followed my gaze. "Huh, she's giving you the stink eye," she said of the heron. "She don't like being stared at, especially by a stranger."

This seemed a surprising side of Dolores. It didn't fit with her reputation. It was hard to imagine tenderness of any kind in her heart, but then again, she had raised Robbie-Lee and he was the nicest man I ever met. Go figure.

"Dolores," I said, trying to get back to the problem at hand. "What do you expect me to do about it? About Darryl, I mean?"

"Don't you go rushing me, girl," Dolores snapped. Her raised voice was met with two sharp squawks, like warning shots, from the heron.

"Aw, will you just stop worrying yourself to death?" Dolores called to the bird. "Do you think I'm going to cook you for my supper? If I was going to do that, I'd have done it already."

"Dolores, look, I want to help, but I don't know if I can stop Darryl," I said. "I'm just one person, and I haven't even lived here the past year, and —"

She hurled her whittling to the ground and jumped up with clenched fists, her arms flailing like a toddler having a tantrum. For a split second I thought she might run straight for me and strangle the life out of me, so I stepped backward, tripping over my suitcase and landing on my rear end. The heron, apparently unhappy with the commotion, burst from its nest, wings a-flapping, in what struck me as an almost-perfect imitation of Dolores.

"You can't let him do this!" Dolores screamed. Half sprawled in the sand, I felt like a turtle that finds itself upside down. I heard the sound of fast-moving footsteps heading away from me — thank you, Jesus. A door slammed, and I felt momentarily relieved. She'd gone inside.

Then it dawned on me that I was in a fine pickle. Soon it would be dark in the swamp, and I wasn't about to walk back to the Tamiami Trail with no flashlight or torch. Moonbeams had a way of illuminating sandy paths that weren't visible during the daytime, making it easy to get confused — and lost — at night.

I'd been so eager to talk to Dolores I'd scurried right over to see her, right off the bus. I guess I thought she'd invite me inside and we'd talk. It hadn't occurred to me that we'd have a big fuss and she'd leave me outside all night.

The fall had knocked the wind out of my lungs. I spent several long moments just looking around me. Dolores had made some improvements to the fishing shack since her son had left home. The front door, if you could call it that, had been painted shocking pink. A hand-carved sign, stuck in the ground and tilting wildly like a forgotten grave-marker, read Home Sweet Home. Off to the right, brush had been cleared away from the outhouse which now featured the words "Powder Room" painted in a girlish script.

But the 'Glades were coming alive with evening sounds. I soon decided that gators, snakes, and panthers were, in fact, scarier than Dolores — although frankly I wasn't 100 percent sure. I struggled back to my feet and edged my way carefully along the dock toward the shack, which sat like a little island on rough-hewn pilings. As I knocked, I ducked to one side, just in case she answered with a shotgun blast.

When she didn't respond, I called out, hoping she could hear me. "Dolores, you know I can't stay out here all night. I need to borrow a flashlight."

Nothing. Quiet as a grave.

I tried again. "Dolores, what would Robbie-Lee say if he knew you weren't looking after me?"

The latch clicked and the door swung open.

"Don't you go saying my son's name," Dolores said. "He ain't here anyway. He up and left me. Went to New York City."

"He'll be back," I said gently. "He's young, and just wanted to see a little more of the world. Just like I did."

"See the world," she harrumphed. "I guess the 'Glades ain't good enough for the likes of you, or him." She paused. "Why would anyone in his right mind go to New York City?"

I couldn't argue with her on that point. Mississippi wasn't exactly a stone's throw away, but at least it was the South.

I noticed she had a drink in her hand. I wasn't sure if this was a good sign or not. "You must hear from him — right? Does he send letters? He should be sending letters," I said, taking her side.

"Yes, he writes me letters but he doesn't tell me much of anything. Says a whole lot of nothing in them letters. Just things about pretty parks and big, tall buildings." Suddenly, she brightened. "He saw Liz Taylor outside some theater on Broadway."

"Really?" I asked, forgetting my problems. "Robbie-Lee saw Elizabeth Taylor in person?"

"Yes, he did," Dolores replied proudly. "She was going to see a play, and he said he was maybe ten feet from her, with him working in the theater and all."

"Well, ain't that something?" I said. "Was she just as purty in person? Did he say in the letter?"

"Oh, purtier!" Dolores replied, as certain as if she'd been there herself. "Can you imagine seeing a Hollywood person like

26

Elizabeth Taylor in the flesh?"

"She was my mama's favorite movie star," I said softly.

"Mine, too," Dolores said wistfully. "Ever since I saw her in *Father of the Bride.*"

Now I was really seeing another side of Dolores Simpson. I had trouble imagining Dolores in a movie theater at all, let alone watching such a sweet and charming movie. Of course, that film had come out fourteen years ago, in 1950, and it made me wonder what Dolores must have been like when she was younger. Then I had a memory of Mama, talking about forgiveness and how hard it was for her to get past the fact that Elizabeth Taylor stole someone else's husband. My mind was a thousand miles away when suddenly I realized Dolores was peering at me as if she'd never really seen me before. All this talk about Elizabeth Taylor had altered the air we were breathing.

"Come in," she said finally.

The next morning I woke up on an ancient horse-hair couch that smelled like spilled beer, stale cigarettes, and low tide. An old metal spring was poking into my back.

She had left me a note, written in pencil in all capital letters. THIS HERE CORN-BREAD IS FOR YOU. TAKE IT AND

27

EAT. TAKE A COKE, TOO. SORRY IT BE WARM. COME BACK AFTER YOU'VE TALKED TO DARRYL.

Talk to Darryl? Oh Lord, in my disoriented state, I'd almost forgotten. Honestly, I'd rather have met the devil before daylight but I had agreed the night before that this was the next step. If it was true that he was going to pave over this part of the 'Glades, I needed to hear it from the horse's mouth. And give him a piece of my mind.

And find out where he got the money to pull off such an idea.

And find a way to stop it. Or at least, keep it from happening right here.

I washed down the cornbread with Coke and was revived enough to start walking back to the Trail. I noticed, as I left, that the mama night heron was using the Home Sweet Home sign for a perch. She stared at me warily as I walked past. I was tempted to say howdy but thought better of it. Poor thing had been through our ruckus the night before. As Mama used to say, "When it comes to Nature, leave it be."

The thick smell of the 'Glades made me feel drugged or a little feverish. I wasn't used to the overwhelming clash of plant life anymore, some of it quite stinky in its own right but bunched together, almost nauseat-

28

ing. Mixed in was a vague scent of decay, helped along by humidity that was almost indescribable, though a high-school friend had come close when he said it felt like being caught in a downpour, only it was raining up. On particularly hot days, Jackie, in her wry Northern way, would say, "How refreshing! Essence of Swamp!" which was funny but always made me feel inferior. However, having been away for a year, I could see her point.

As I marched along, I tried to picture my friend Robbie-Lee making this same trek day after day for years, just to get to school or the library or anywhere. And I wondered how in the world he had survived growing up with Dolores as his mother.

After disturbing several snakes along the way, I finally reached the Trail where, mercifully, I got a ride from a truck driver heading south to Everglades City. I guess I was a pathetic sight, walking down the side of the road with a suitcase in my hand. I offered him a dollar when he dropped me off by the Esso station, but he wouldn't take it. Told me I'd better take good care of myself, and that's when I realized that I must've looked like death warmed over in a saucepan. I didn't want anyone else to see me like that. Pride is a sin and so is vanity, but who wants to return to her hometown looking like a wilted orchid?

It was still early, and Naples was not fully stirring. I walked quick as I could, hoping I wouldn't run into anyone. It was already hot as Hades, and I had to catch my breath twice. While I was confident that Judd Hart, Jackie's teenage son, had been taking good care of my pet turtles, I was eager to see them. I managed to half run the last hundred yards to my little cottage with my little suitcase bumping against my thigh at every step.

I opened the gate and stepped into the yard. Nothing stirred, so I whistled and stayed still. I whistled a second time and heard some rustling. Slowly, they came out from their hiding places, their heads poking out, curious. And then they lumbered toward me, picking up speed, with Norma Jean, always the boss, in the lead. When they got close they stopped short. They didn't have the greatest eyesight in the world but as soon as they heard my voice they knew it was me.

I wanted to spend the next hour right there in the front yard but I had to go inside and pull myself together. Happily, the cottage did not need airing out. Judd had clearly been following my instructions.

I unpacked my suitcase and showered. Only then did I allow myself to settle into Mama's favorite chair. How I missed her. In the year I had spent away I had often imagined sitting in her chair and feeling comforted, and I did. But I also felt a deep stab of sadness.

I was born right here in this little cottage. There wasn't a nickel to spare for a doctor, not that there was usually one available, especially with the Depression going on. Thankfully, Mama had been trained as a nurse and so she birthed me herself.

Mama used to say that at least Daddy left us with a roof over our heads. Not that it was much of a roof. Every time we had a hurricane it leaked in a new and mysterious way, and Mama and I would spend the duration of the storm moving mop buckets from place to place until we were too tired to care. The year I turned fifteen, Mama finally had enough money set aside from her part-time nursing jobs to have it fixed proper.

When I married Darryl, a local boy I'd known since childhood, we set up house-keeping all the way up in Ocala. I wasn't happy about it, but Darryl had landed a good construction job. Before long Mama took sick, and I began spending more time with her in Naples than with Darryl in Ocala.

That's when I found out that Darryl had a mean streak. He didn't like me being away from him, even for a good reason. The sicker Mama got, the more petty and irritated Darryl became. Later, I spent a lot of time trying to decide if he'd changed overnight or if he'd always been that way and I had failed to notice.

Mama and I both thought she had glade fever and it would pass once the weather turned. But even when the rains ended, she was still feeling puny. I knew things were bad when she gave up all her part-time nursing jobs, one by one, including her favorite, her twice-daily visit to check on Miss Maude Mobley, who was ninety-three and lived alone. Miss Mobley had outlived all her friends and kin. She didn't need to be in a state home; she just needed someone like Mama to make sure she was taking her liver pills and eating proper. Mama wouldn't rest easy until I went to Miss Mobley's church and asked the preacher to find someone to take Mama's place.

Not that anyone could take Mama's place. I always knew that was the case, but imagining and living it are two different things. Her final decline happened sooner than I expected. Without telling me, Mama slipped out one morning while I was shopping at the Winn-Dixie. She took the bus to Fort Myers, where she saw a blood doctor. When she came home, she told me she had cancer and they couldn't fix it. Two weeks after Mama saw the doctor in Fort Myers, she crossed over to the Spirit World in her sleep.

After the burial, I went up to Ocala, packed up my things, and came home. Now it was just me at the little cottage on the Gulf. Me and my turtles.

Returning home to Naples as a divorced woman was even harder than I thought it would be. People I'd known my whole life — even old pals from school — avoided me. I got a job at the post office and was thankful for it, but on the days I was assigned to counter duty I found myself having to make small talk with people who looked down on me. If not for Jackie Hart and her book club, I'd have remained friendless.

These memories were exhausting, and I was tempted to let myself fall asleep in Mama's chair. The deep, soft cushions still smelled of her.

But my mind was too restless. Part of me wanted to handle Darryl on my own to show everyone that little Dora Witherspoon was more independent and confident than she used to be. This was plain foolishness, however, and I could practically feel Mama glaring down at me from the Other Side. Mama would have said there was no shame in asking for help, in which case I had only one place to turn: my old book club. If anyone could stop Darryl, it was the members of the Collier County Women's Literary Society. Especially, an outspoken woman from Boston named Jackie Hart.

FOUR

Dolores Simpson sat on the dock that led to her fishing shack and wondered how she'd ended up here, alone, on the edge of the 'Glades with no one to talk to except a nervous night heron. Nothing in her life had gone right. She wasn't even sure who she was anymore. Truth be told, she wasn't even Dolores Simpson.

Her real name was Bunny Ann McIntyre. She always wondered what her mama had been thinking when she wrote those words in the family Bible. Of course, when she became a grown girl and was working as a stripper (she preferred "fan dancer") in Tampa, Bunny was a perfectly suitable name. At least she didn't have to come up with something new and catchy like all the other girls. The funny thing was, girls named Mary, Elizabeth, and Susan who became Safire, Sugar, or Bubbles were annoyed that she was, in fact, an actual Bunny. Why this

35

bothered them was a mystery to her, but then women in general had always seemed more complicated than men.

When she fled from that life and moved back to the Everglades, she wanted a new name to go with a new life. On the bus heading south from Hillsborough County, a lady in a tailored navy suit left a magazine on the seat next to her. Dolores picked it up and flipped to a random page where she began reading about a woman named Dolores Simpson who owned a six-bedroom home, an Olympic-sized swimming pool, a maid, and even a Lincoln Continental. And she hadn't done it by marrying some man. No, according to the story, she had started her own business. She was even quoted as saying she *didn't need* a man in her life. Incredible! How she wished she could be that woman, and if she couldn't, well, at least she could borrow her name.

Good-bye, "Bunny." Hello, "Dolores."

But a lot of good it had done her.

She spat a stream of tobacco juice, taking care not to hit the pink bougainvillea that Robbie-Lee had planted at the foot of the dock. Dolores had learned the hard way that bougainvillea, which was generally quite hardy, would shrivel up and die if it had an unlucky encounter with tobacco spit. While she wasn't partial to flowers, Dolores couldn't see the sense in ruining a perfectly good plant. Besides, Robbie-Lee was fond of it, and she wanted it to be here looking purty when he came back.

If he came back.

"*Oooh,* my son is gone. Gone to see the world," she moaned softly. Adding, "Fool. Dang fool."

She wished she could direct that nasty stream of tobacco juice right at the feet of the folks who had created her problems. First was Jackie Hart, that trouble-making redhead from Boston. Robbie-Lee had been doing just fine until Jackie came along. The boy had a promising future which he now had thrown away. He'd managed to get hisself the rarest kind of job, one in which he didn't get his hands dirty. As the sole employee for Sears, Roebuck & Company in Collier County, he'd helped folks place their orders from the catalog. It didn't matter that the Sears Center where he worked was the size of an ice cream stand. He wore nice clothes to work and he wasn't going to age overnight the way most of the menfolk in Collier did, either from the fishing industry or farming melons and sugarcane.

But then all of a sudden he left for New York City. Just like that. New York City!

Inspired by that awful woman, Jackie Hart, who put it in his head that he was missing something. Well, dagnabbit, if he wanted to go north so badly he could have gone to Fort Myers, or Sarasota, or maybe even Apalachicola. At least he would have still been in Florida. He'd have still been squarely on Confederate turf. But why New York City? It wasn't even part of the United States, as far as Dolores was concerned.

She looked over at the night heron. "Oh, just you wait and see," Dolores said mournfully. "Being a mother is hard. When they grow up, they gonna do what they gonna do. Your young'uns will do the same to you that my boy did to me.

"But he'll be back one day," she added, this time to herself. "I know he will."

The second person who had messed up her life was Darryl Norwood, ex-husband of that little gal, Dora Witherspoon. She hoped she'd gotten through to Dora. The telegram had worked to bring her back here. Maybe there was some hope that the river could be saved.

If not, she would have nowhere to go. "Things won't be so peachy for you, either," she called over to the bird. "You're going to be the last night heron in Collier County. What we have here is a mighty bad situation. At least you can fly away. You can start over. I can't. I'm good for nothin'. I'm stuck."

Dolores examined her hands. Twenty-five years working in the 'Glades, and they looked like the skin of the alligators she caught. But that was the least of her worries. Back when she'd been a dancer, the owner of the club had complained that her breasts were too small. Unless she allowed liquid filler to be injected into her breasts, she would lose her job. She'd gone along with it. Now they were lumpy, and hard, and hurt in ways she didn't think possible. How stupid she'd been when she was young. Some mistakes you pay for, forever.

Her first mistake was thinking she was in love. She was fifteen and had just finished eighth grade. When her belly started swelling, she thought maybe she had worms, or possibly a hernia. But her mama and daddy knew otherwise. They threw her out.

She'd hitchhiked to Tampa on the back of a tomato truck in pouring rain. She still didn't know what was wrong with her or why her parents made her leave, but a stranger on the streets of Tampa took one look at her and walked her to a hospital emergency room. Three hours later she had her baby. The nuns convinced her she was racked by sin and not worthy to be a mother. She never had a chance to hold the baby. She wasn't even sure if the baby was alive or healthy, and there were times when she wondered if she had dreamed the whole thing.

She left that hospital four days later on her own two feet, alone. She hitchhiked to the beach in St. Pete and survived by stealing picnics from tourists. Being so young, her body bounced back quickly, and soon she got herself a job at a nightclub. It was only after she showed up on her first day of work that she found out she was to be a dancer, not a waitress. She went along with it, thinking she'd do it just for a while, but "a while" turned into seven years. And that's when she got pregnant again.

The owner of the nightclub suggested an option that would, as he said, "fix" the situation but Dolores was too scared to consider it. One of the other dancers — a sweet-faced girl from Alabama — had gone to an underground clinic and died.

Surrendering another baby to the State of Florida was out of the question, as far as Dolores was concerned. This baby was a keeper, come what may. She had him at the same hospital as the first one, only this time she was prepared. She scooped him up and took off out of there before somebody could thrust papers in her face and hand her a pen. She named him Robbie-Lee after a crop reporter she liked to listen to on the radio. A man who sounded nice, day in and day out, whether he was discussing the worrisome possibility of a January freeze in the orange groves or warning listeners about a fierce storm that had popped up over the Gulf on a summer day. Sometimes the friendly voice asked questions which he quickly answered himself. For example: *Did you know that Tampa is the lightning capital of the United States?* (Well, it is!) Or: *Did you know that many historians believe our city gets its name from the Calusa Indians, or the Shell People, because "Tampa" means "sticks of fire" in their ancient language?* (Well, it does!) So her radio announcer was smart as well as nice, a quality which Dolores admired.

Within hours of leaving the hospital, she fled the area with Robbie-Lee curled up like a kitten under a silk scarf she'd snatched years earlier from a Canadian traveler, or "snowbird." She skipped out of Dodge without so much as a fare-thee-well to anyone, not wanting to alert her landlord, who would have had her sent to jail for being late on the rent. Never mind that her baby would be taken from her.

All she could think of was to head back down to Collier County. That's what people do when they're almost out of hope, right? Head home? She had heard through the grapevine that her parents were dead, so at least she didn't have to face their scorn again. And Collier County was familiar. As for making a living, her granddaddy had hunted gators in the 'Glades back in the day, and she thought, *Well, heck, I can do that. I watched him do it. I helped him do it.*

Besides, she figured, huntin' gators couldn't be any harder or more dangerous than working in some old strip club. In fact, it might be easier.

The years slipped by like the hidden currents in the river. She wouldn't have said she'd been happy — she wasn't sure what that felt like — but she wasn't miserable. She got by, and folks left her alone. Most importantly, Robbie-Lee had grown up handsome, clever, and nice, just as she'd dreamed.

If only Robbie-Lee had stayed away from that book club he would be here, helping her with the gators. She hated to admit it but she had come to rely on Robbie-Lee to lend a hand with the big, unruly ones. Since he'd left, she'd pretty much given up the gator business altogether. Especially after an odd thing happened: She had started feeling sorry for the critters. She'd never sympathized with the big ones, which would just as soon eat her up, but the little ones — the only kind she could now grab hold of these days — well, they were almost cute! This had come as a shock to her, and she had quietly started retiring her gear.

She was living on fish she could catch from her dock. She sold grunts — minnows, the Yankees called 'em — to the bait shops, always setting aside a healthy portion for herself. She rolled the tiny things in flour and fried 'em up whole, just like her grand-daddy did, and served 'em with a mess of grits. Indeed, there was nothing Dolores liked better than a big ol' plate of grits and grunts.

And now someone wanted to take it all away. To some folks it probably wouldn't have seemed like much. But to her, it was a little slice of heaven.

How could a man grow up in the 'Glades and fail to see its beauty? How could he look at it and see only money? She'd run into plenty of men like Darryl in her life. They thought of no one other than them-selves. They weren't any different from the school-yard bullies who used to pick on

Robbie-Lee, calling him "homo" and other names. Darryl and those just like him, she decided, were evil.

The person who was harder to understand was Jackie. She had a nice home, a husband with a steady job, a couple of kids, and a Buick convertible. What else could a woman want? *If I had that kind of life,* Dolores thought wistfully, *I would be busy living it. I wouldn't waste my time creating problems and meddling in other people's business.*

Dolores had never met anyone from Boston and wondered if they were all like Jackie. First of all, that peculiar accent that was near impossible to understand. Plus the bizarre urge to speak your mind and have everything upfront and out in the open. And the worst Yankee trait of all, a missionary zeal to fix everything Southern.

Not that Jackie was a bad person. She wasn't evil like Darryl. She was just a Yankee and, typical of the Northern born, couldn't leave well enough alone.

FIVE

"There's something I need to tell you, Miss Witherspoon," Judd Hart was saying, and I noticed he wouldn't look me in the eye. When he heard I was back in town, Judd made a beeline to my cottage to say hello. With his red hair and blue eyes, it was easy to see that he was Jackie's son. He was thirteen now and about four inches taller than when I left. We were sitting on the bottom step of my porch, feeding pieces of honeydew melon to my snappers. Of course, this meant having to scold Norma Jean from time to time. She was such a piggy, and I could see she hadn't changed a bit.

"Judd," I said, "you don't have to call me Miss Witherspoon. You can call me Dora."

"I can't call you Dora. You're a grown-up."

"Well, then, call me Miss Dora," I said.

Judd frowned. I guess that was too Southern.

"Well," I prompted him, "what is it you want to tell me?" I tried to hide the nervousness from my voice. "Is it about all this business with my former husband and the development he wants to build?"

"No, not that," Judd said. "I just wanted to warn you that when you see my mom, she'll look a little, um, different."

All I could think of was that maybe Jackie had changed her hair, or gained weight.

Judd looked away. "She'll be wearing black," he mumbled.

"What?"

"Black. You know, mourning clothes."

"Oh, Judd! Someone in your family went to Glory? No one told me! I'm so sorry! Who was it?" My heart went into a tailspin of pity and sorrow. Poor Jackie!

"Well, no one in our . . . family." Judd looked miserable.

"Then . . . who?" I asked.

"President Kennedy."

Hmmm. Jackie had been wearing mourning clothes — for President Kennedy? Since the previous November? In three months it would be a year. I had figured she took it hard but I didn't think she would carry on this long.

"She says she's going to wear them for one year and a day," Judd went on. "I just didn't want you to be surprised."

"Judd, let me ask you something, and it might seem like a silly question," I said. "You know I've never been up north. What I want to know is, is this something all Yankees do?" In my head, I was picturing everyone in Boston walking around in black.

"Nope," Judd said. "I don't think so. I'm pretty sure she's the only one in America, other than the Kennedy family, of course. This is just Mom being Mom."

"Oh," I said, at a loss for words. So wearing black for a year, for a president not everyone liked (especially in the South), would be considered odd even in Boston. There were times like this when I got a hint that Jackie was over the top even for a Yankee. "Well," I said, finally finding my voice, "as the saying goes, 'To each his own.'"

Judd suddenly seemed defensive. "I guess with her being from Boston and all, and she's such a fan of Mrs. Kennedy, and all that . . ." His voice trailed off. He tried to grin but it came off as a lame little smile, so he shrugged instead. "I didn't want you to be, you know, caught off guard. Because when I told her I'd heard you were back in town, she ran to get dressed and I know she's headed over here any minute now."

We'd run out of melon strips to give the turtles. Castro and Myrtle had gone into the shrubs to take naps. Norma Jean was still begging for goodies. She stared at us and made munching movements with her mouth. "Yes, we see you, Norma Jean," I said, laughing. It was hard to miss an Everglades snapping turtle the size of Mama's divan.

"You know what, Judd?" I said. "You've done a fine job here, looking after my friends."

Judd beamed at my compliment. "I really mean that," I added. "I wouldn't have gone off to Mississippi if you hadn't been here to take care of my turtles. And check on my little cottage. But everything looks swell. Did you have any problems?"

"No, ma'am," he said, and I was pleased to hear the "ma'am" roll off his tongue, since a Boston boy wouldn't survive down here for long if he didn't learn the basics. Seems like he'd settled in fairly good.

And then he asked me a question I didn't know the answer to. "How long are you going to be back for?"

"I don't know, Judd." I sighed before continuing. "I've still got something I need to do back in Mississippi. But I've got to see if I can help Robbie-Lee's mother. She's

48

going to lose her home if my stupid former husband" — I paused for a moment, regretting that I had referred to Darryl in such a mean-spirited way in front of Judd — "uh, if my former husband fills in the swamp over there."

Judd was quiet for a moment. "But where would all the turtles, and the gators and everything, go?" he asked.

I was thinking Judd might be a great ally when we both heard brakes squeal. Before you could say "Sweet Jesus, protect me from whatever that is," Jackie's convertible slid to a halt in the wind-driven sand that always seemed to pile up on the street directly in front of my cottage. There was no one else in Naples who drove quite like that. And, there was no other car like that south of Tampa: a completely impractical, two-door, banana-yellow 1960 Buick LeSabre for which she had traded, in a moment of pure rebellion, her dull and matronly station wagon.

We loved that car. Oh, how we all loved it. No one else in our book club owned a car, and Jackie had enjoyed driving us around. It was wonderful to see her again, right behind the wheel, which is how I usually pictured her in my mind although the effect was altered somewhat since she was indeed wearing black. A black head scarf. Black gloves. Black cat-eye sunglasses. And, of course, a black dress that was tasteful but not especially demure. Probably, from that store she was always talking about, Filene's.

Black is not an easy color to wear in Florida under the best of circumstances and, in Naples, it was always a signal that someone had up and died. Black was for grieving and condoling only. Of course, that might not have been true, say, in Miami or some other place where they had bona fide nightclubs. Here in Naples the only place was the Shingle Shack, and I doubt any woman ever wore black unless she was coming straight from the kind of funeral that drives a woman to drink.

Jackie leaned on the car horn, a Yankee habit that made me want to reach for smelling salts. Why in the name of Our Sweet Savior did she think this was necessary? Did she think we couldn't see her? She was smiling and waving her arm with the kind of jaunty Northern confidence that annoys the beeswax out of Southerners. Plain Jane, the poet from our book club, was sprawled in the backseat like she was sunbathing on a chaise lounge. I almost hadn't noticed her.

"Woo hoo!" I called out, once I had recovered from the car horn. "So great to see y'all! Git yourselves out of that crazy car and come set on the porch with me and Judd for a spell!" But as soon as I raised my voice, I could feel Mama's disapproval coming straight down from the Spirit World like a bolt of lightning, since hollerin' was "not nice." Mama was always talking about things that were either "nice" or "not nice." That was pretty much how she saw the world. Judd, Jackie, and Plain Jane were probably wondering why I sprang up, rabbit-like, rather than shout again, but I knew better than to disrespect Mama. It didn't matter than she was six feet under at the Cemetery of Hope and Salvation over by the Esso station.

Jackie and Plain Jane had both climbed out of the car, and I thought we were going to have a bear-hug reunion, but when I got to the gate and started fussing with the latch, Jackie started screeching like a banshee on a coconut-milk binge. "Don't open it!" she pleaded.

I had plumb forgot that Jackie was scared to pieces of my turtles. It was a wonder she let Judd look after them while I was away. For the sake of friendship, and to keep Jackie calm, I climbed over my own fence. Jackie, Plain Jane, and me had a three-way hug like a football huddle. You know you like someone, and truly missed them, when you don't mind embracing them in the suffocating heat of Florida in August.

I wasn't sure about other book clubs, but making a decision, even with just three of us present, required more discussion than Khrushchev and Kennedy probably had during the entire Cuban Missile Crisis. Plain Jane wanted to sit on my porch and sip iced tea and get caught up. Jackie balked on account of my turtles which (a little rudely, in my opinion) she kept referring to as "those dreadful things." She suggested we go to her house and drink mimosas. I knew what I wanted to do, but I waited for the two of them to talk their ideas to death. Finally, there was a lull. "Where's the baby?" I asked. "I'm dying to see her."

Instantly, it was agreed that we would all go to Mrs. Bailey White's house, where the baby spent most of her time.

Judd was obviously relieved that we were leaving. Jackie called to him, "Honey, I made some chili for you and the twins. Go ahead and eat if I'm not home in time for supper. And there's a special honeydew melon that I bought just for you."

As we were driving away, two things occurred to me. One was that the aforementioned honeydew melon was, in all likeli-

frankly, almost scared me more) until we were close enough to pull up a few feet from him. I could see that he recognized the car — of course he did. Everyone in southwest Florida knew that car.

"Excuse me, *sir,*" Jackie said, like she was about to ask for directions.

I almost felt sorry for Darryl. He was entirely flummoxed. "I thought I heard a car horn a while ago," he said. "I guess that was you?"

"Might have been," Jackie said with that same edge to her voice.

"You're Miss Dreamsville, aren't you?" he asked. "Mrs. Jackie Hart?"

"Yes," she said icily.

"Oh, I see you're in mourning. I'm sorry for your loss."

"And I see that you have chosen to call your development 'Dreamsville.' The implication is that I am endorsing this project. You will be hearing from my attorney."

This was a side to Jackie I hadn't seen. Although she was so mad I sensed she was quivering beside me, she had reined in her temper.

"Well, actually, it's going to be called Dreamsville Estates," Darryl said without emotion. "Our slogan is Welcome to Dreamsville!"

"What nerve you have!" Jackie said, struggling to maintain her dignity. "I am aghast! Never have I seen such audacity!"

Darryl smirked. "All's fair —"

"— in love and war?" Jackie said, finishing the old saying for him.

"And — when it comes to Florida real estate," he added. "But you wouldn't know that, would you? Since you're not from around here."

"I'm not brand-new here," she snapped. "I've lived here for two years."

"Well, whoop-dee-do," Darryl said. "Two whole years. Lady, if you lived here for twenty years, you'd still be an outsider."

"Go ahead and laugh at me, sir," Jackie said, lighting a cigarette and blowing a stream of smoke directly into his face. "You will be sorry."

"Is that a *threat*?" Darryl asked, pretending to be taken aback.

"Take it any way you like," she said, "but don't say I didn't warn you. Never underestimate a woman from Boston, or do so at your own peril. Oh," she added, suddenly remembering I was there. "I believe that Dora here" — she gestured to the passenger seat — "would like to have a word with you before we leave."

Darryl leaned down and looked in amazement at me, hunkered against the far door. "Dora!" he said, clearly stunned. "What are you doing way out here?"

I took this as my cue. My knees were wobbly, but I got out of the car. Now was the time. I was hoping Jackie would understand that I needed to be alone with Darryl for a few minutes, and despite her distress, she got the hint. "Dora, shall I come back later?" she asked.

"No, Jackie," I said quickly. "Just wait here." We weren't at the Dairy Queen, for pity's sake, and while I wasn't particularly afraid of Darryl, I didn't want to be stuck out here with him, either. She nodded and moved the car a respectful distance away.

"Do you want to talk in the trailer?" Darryl said, still looking shocked. "Or we can talk in my truck."

"Truck is fine," I said. I could tell he was having trouble reading my mood. Angry? Sad? What? Well, the truth was that I was nervous as a rabbit at a hound dog convention but I was determined to hide it.

He opened the door for me, then went around to the driver's side and climbed in. The windows were lowered already, or the truck would have been hot enough to fry bacon. Even so, the seats were roasting.

"Dang, it's hot," Darryl said, buying time.

"Surely is."

"It's *really* hot."

"Darryl, I need to talk to you about something other than the weather."

"Okay," he said. "I thought you were in Mississippi. I didn't even know you were back."

I cut to the chase. "Darryl, why are you doing this?"

"Doing what?"

"Ruining the swamp! Paving over the river! And on top of it, calling it Dreamsville! That's not fair to my friend!"

Darryl laughed. "You came all this way to fuss at me about that?! Let me tell you something, Dora, you're just as nutty as your friend there. If you'd stayed with me, you could have been a rich woman."

"Darryl, what in tarnation has happened to your *soul*?"

"Oh, so now it's my soul we're talking about. Gee, Dora, I never thought of you as being the Bible-thumping type. You trying to get me back to church? You weren't there yourself every Sunday, if I remember correctly."

We had fallen back into our old pattern, the kind of fighting that makes you get madder and madder and gets you nowhere. "Darryl, let's stay on the topic," I said, trying to sound calm and mature, although I surely didn't feel that way. "You and me — we grew up around here. We played here. You helped me rescue turtles, do you remember that? I knew you had changed. That's why I couldn't stay married to you anymore. But this — this *development* — well, I'm shocked, Darryl. Not only are you going to wipe out the animals and the birds, there are people living here, too. They don't have anywhere else to go. If you do this, Darryl, there's no going back. The 'Glades have been here forever; you're going to change that?"

Darryl was silent. "There's a lot more 'Glades than just the part I want to build on," he said finally. "This is just one piece of the 'Glades. Besides, if I don't build on it, someone else will. Trust me on that, Dora."

"Well, I don't trust you, Darryl. And it makes me very sad to say that."

"So you came here to try to persuade me to change my mind?"

"Well, yes, Darryl. I thought it was worth a try. For old times' sake."

"There's something you should know, Dora," he said, and his voice sounded different. "I was going to write to you in Mississippi. I'm getting married."

"I see," I said as calmly as I could manage. I wanted to say, *Well, that was quick, Darryl,* but I curbed my tongue. "Oh," I managed to say faintly. "Well, good for you, Darryl. What's her name?"

"Celeste," he said, without providing a last name. "I met her in New York on a business trip. Well, her folks live in New Jersey. In Basking Ridge."

Basking Ridge, I thought. I couldn't remember where I'd heard that before but at the moment it didn't matter. "That's nice, Darryl," I said simply. "Thank you. I mean, thank you for telling me." I suddenly felt tears stinging the corners of my eyes. Did this mean I still loved him? Or were they tears of a different kind — humiliation that we had failed as a couple and he had found someone new? I climbed out of the truck without looking at him, hoping he wouldn't see. As I walked back to Jackie's car, though, I realized he was following me. I figured he just wanted to get the last word. All I wanted to do was hightail it out of there.

"Dora, you shouldn't judge me!" he said, and now he sounded angry. He was right on my heels. "Aren't you going to wish me good luck on my marriage?" This was said with so much bile that I was sorely tempted to turn around and slap him.

"Now, you two settle down," Jackie called out. She must have heard the last exchange of words, maybe more. I kept my stride steady and marched to the passenger side, got in, and locked the door.

He muttered and fumed, then surprised me by turning and walking around to Jackie's side of the car. "You know what?" he shouted in Jackie's face. "If it hadn't been for you and your *Miss Dreamsville* radio show, I wouldn't have been able to get the financing. You put us on the map! So thank you very much for helping me get rich!"

Jackie looked stricken. She opened her mouth but no words came out. Darryl turned his back and stomped arrogantly toward his truck. A second later he was gone, tearing down the road at a reckless speed.

I wondered if he knew how lucky he was. After taunting Jackie, he had walked right in front of her car. If she had recovered faster, my former husband could easily have become a brand-new hood ornament on the flashiest car in town.

ELEVEN

"I hope Seminole Joe catches up to him," Mrs. Bailey White said. We were sitting in her parlor, having skedaddled from Darryl's construction site for a place to talk things out. Jackie was worn out, collapsed on Mrs. Bailey White's good sofa after a marathon weeping session that was fueled by pure rage and peppered with threats and oaths about high-powered Northern lawyers and what they would do to Darryl for having the nerve to steal her name.

"Who is Seminole Joe?" Jackie asked wearily.

Mrs. Bailey White and I locked eyes, and Plain Jane, slouched in an oversized leather chair near the fireplace, looked up from the book she was reading and chuckled softly.

"What's so funny?" Jackie demanded.

"Nothin'," Plain Jane said, returning to her book.

"Seminole Joe is a haint," I said simply. I

was sitting on the floor, trying to get better acquainted with Dream, who was having a good ol' time with a set of alphabet blocks that Plain Jane had purchased at the Junior League yard sale.

"A ghost," Mrs. Bailey White added, translating for Jackie.

I didn't want to get onto the topic of Seminole Joe, not after the day I'd had, and surely not in Mrs. Bailey White's parlor, where her kinfolk were lined up in jars on the mantel. Or, rather, the ashes of her kinfolk. The way I was raised — along with just about everyone else in Collier County — your body was supposed to be buried, not reduced to dust and placed in your home *on the mantelpiece* like a 4-H trophy. I had never got myself used to their presence.

But Jackie, being Jackie, was not going to be satisfied with our skirting the topic. "I never heard of this 'Seminole Joe' before," she said crossly. "Is this some kind of local secret?"

"Seminole Joe is our boogeyman," I said simply. I watched as Dream toppled the blocks by piling on one too many. She chuckled and clapped her hands in delight. "Maybe," I added, "we shouldn't talk about Seminole Joe until Dream has her nap."

"She's too young to understand what we're talking about," Jackie said.

"I wouldn't count on that," said Plain Jane, looking up from her book again. "It's time for her nap, anyway," she added. "I'll take her up."

"So, who is this Seminole Joe person?" Jackie asked again.

"As I said, he's Collier County's very own boogeyman," I replied.

"I hate that term, 'boogeyman,' " Jackie said, lighting a cigarette. "And I don't believe in ghosts," she added between puffs.

"You live around here long enough, you'll believe in 'em," Mrs. Bailey White said under her breath.

"Well, what does this have to do with Darryl?" Jackie asked. "You said something about Seminole Joe catching up to Darryl. It may not be necessary after my lawyer gets through with him."

"Oh, it was just wishful thinking," Mrs. Bailey White said. "I mean, that would solve all our problems."

Jackie said nothing. I could see she was taking this all in, though how she was interpreting it, I wasn't sure.

"Don't you want to know who Seminole Joe was, I mean *is*?" I asked.

"Okay, I'll bite," Jackie said.

I looked at Mrs. Bailey White. Since she brought up the subject, it was her story to tell.

Mrs. Bailey White took a ladylike sip of iced tea, cleared her throat, and began. "A long time ago, when white folks first showed up here, the Indians didn't know what to think," she said in a tone that reminded me of a schoolteacher talking to her pupils. "They were Spanish, and they showed up one day in their sailing ships. Before long they discovered there was a fresh-water spring on Marco Island and they'd stop there, regular-like, on their way to whatever they were doing. Exploring, I guess, but also raisin' Cain.

"Anyway, an Indian named Joe was killed by a pirate. Some say the murderer was the famous pirate Gasparilla, but no one knows for sure. After that, the ghost of this poor Indian fellow, Joe, started to attack them in their sleep and feed their body parts to the alligators. Or so the story went. After a while, the Spanish started avoiding Marco Island and the area we call Collier County altogether. As long as they stayed away, Joe was at peace.

"During the War of Northern Aggression, deserters from both sides — Mr. Lincoln's army as well as our Rebs — found their way to South Florida. They hung deserters in those days. The more skeert they were of getting caught, the farther south they ran. So here in Collier County we had the worst ones — the kind that had gone plumb jack crazy. In the First World War, they called it 'shell shock' but I'm not sure they had a name for it back in Mr. Lincoln's War. And that's when the stories about Joe's ghost started up again. From that time on, folks started referring to him as Seminole Joe.

"If you were in the swamp after dark, he might come after you with a hatchet. Lots of folks went missing on account of old Joe. He didn't seem to bother the Negroes. He only went after the whites. Especially our Confederate soldiers, because they reminded him of General Andrew Jackson from South Carolina. If there was one person the Seminole Indians hated, it was General Jackson. Before Jackson became President of the United States, he made his name fighting the Seminoles. To this very day, don't ever hand a twenty-dollar bill to a Seminole Indian or he will refuse it and spit on the ground, because Andrew Jackson's picture is on the twenty-dollar bill."

Mrs. Bailey White paused for dramatic effect, then went on.

"Old-time Collier County folks don't like

to talk about Seminole Joe because it was considered bad luck to say his name aloud. He was still roaming around when I was a young girl. The most famous case in my day was when a moonshiner named Gerry Brevard made the mistake of setting up his equipment right where Seminole Joe and his people are buried. Normally, Seminole Joe wouldn't bother with a loser like Gerry Brevard but Seminole Indians are mighty particular about their burial grounds. Gerry Brevard had to go.

"My daddy and Judge Harvey P. Decker are the ones who found him. He ran straight out into the road, and they almost hit him, but he was half-dead anyway. In his final breaths, he pointed to the swamp and said, 'Seminole Joe.' There was a sound in the swamp and my daddy looked up and there he was — the old Indian haint hisself, watching them. Next thing they heard was Gerry Brevard's rattle of death, so they turned their attention to him. When they looked back at the swamp a moment later, Seminole Joe had vanished."

Mrs. Bailey White picked up her knitting, which was her way of letting us know she had finished her story. Jackie looked at me, started to say something, but changed her mind. I was trying to hide my excitement.

Mrs. Bailey White had told the story of Seminole Joe in more detail than I'd ever heard it.

After a few moments of silence, except for the little clicking noises from Mrs. Bailey White's knitting needles, I couldn't stand it any longer. "Mrs. Bailey White," I said breathlessly, "I can't believe you knew someone — your own father — who saw Seminole Joe!"

"Oh, well, I saw him, too," Mrs. Bailey White said, pausing in her knitting. "I was in the car. In the backseat."

"Sweet Jesus!" I said, jumping to my feet.

"Oh, for Pete's sake, Dora, cut it out," Jackie said. "It's just a story."

Plain Jane came back down the stairs, having finally settled Dream for a late nap. "What's going on down here?" she asked. I filled her in, and noticed that she was watching Jackie carefully.

"So, Jackie, what do you think of all this?" Plain Jane asked, although surely she anticipated the answer.

"I don't believe any of it," Jackie declared, "but I suppose it would serve Darryl right if he ran into old Seminole Joe." She laughed at her own little joke.

Mrs. Bailey White and I looked at each other, a little alarmed. No matter what Darryl did, he didn't deserve that fate. Plain Jane, settling back in her favorite chair, sighed and shook her head.

"What book is that you're reading?" I asked, hoping to change the subject.

Plain Jane held up the cover for me to see. "*To the Lighthouse* by Virginia Woolf. I've been hearing about this book for years and years, and then Jackie suggested we read it."

"It's a book club pick?" I said, feeling left out once again. I had wondered if the three members of the club who'd stayed in Naples would keep choosing and discussing books.

"Why, Dora, we should have told you what we've been reading, and you could have been reading it, too," Plain Jane said guiltily.

"It's okay, I read it anyway, a few years ago," I said, adding, "I thought it was beautiful."

"Aw, everyone says they love *To the Lighthouse*," Jackie complained.

"You didn't like it?" I asked, surprised.

"Not as much as the others did," Jackie sniffed. "I think it's one of those books you're *supposed* to love."

"What do you mean?" Plain Jane cried.

"It's one of those books people talk about at cocktail parties," Jackie said. "Everyone trying to sound so *terribly sophisticated* says, 'Oh, *To the Lighthouse* is my favorite!' but half of them haven't even read it."

"Oh, Jackie!" Plain Jane said. "I think you are so wrong. I just read it again and frankly it is unforgettable. There's a passage I'm looking for . . ."

"Dora, Plain Jane is right — shame on us for not letting you know what we were reading," Mrs. Bailey White said. "We just thought you were busy with your adventure in Mississippi and we didn't want to interfere."

"Ah, yes," Jackie said. "Speaking of your adventure in Mississippi, are you going to tell us what you found out about your family?"

"Oh," I said, completely off guard. I started to say something evasively Southern but stopped myself. I could learn *something* from Jackie, couldn't I? So I tried my hand at Jackie's signature bluntness. "I'm not ready to talk about that yet," I said, and although it sounded Yankee-rude it also felt surprisingly good to say what I meant.

The others looked a little surprised. "Well, Dora dear, whenever you're ready," Plain Jane said, rescuing me. "For the moment, we need to figure out what we're going to do about Darryl, anyway."

"What, other than hoping Seminole Joe goes after him?" Jackie chortled. "Seriously, I'm beginning to think that old ghost could help us in some way."

"Jackie, you are going to get us into some serious trouble," Plain Jane said uneasily.

"Oh, don't be silly!" Jackie said, lighting yet another cigarette. "What do you think I'm suggesting? Summoning the ancient spirit of Seminole Joe and asking for his help?"

"Well, I suppose one of us could dress up like Seminole Joe and sneak up and bop Darryl over the head, not to hurt him but just to scare him," Mrs. Bailey White said thoughtfully. "Maybe then he'd be afraid to go ahead with his project?"

I swallowed hard. "I don't think that's funny," I said.

"I wasn't joking," Mrs. Bailey White replied. I looked at her for a long time, trying to reconcile this sweet-looking little old lady with the woman who had done time in jail and was now suggesting that we hit my former husband over the head "just to scare him."

"Mrs. Bailey White," I said, my voice all squeaky and trembling, "this is out of the question, and I do not want to be part of this conversation."

"Oh," Mrs. Bailey White said, looking a little chagrined. "Sorry I upset you, Dora."

"Now, girls," Jackie said, trying to defuse the situation. "I have a better idea. You know how I used to do some copyediting over at the newspaper, before I had my radio show? Well, I've been asked to do some writing — a column, as a matter of fact!"

"How exciting!" Plain Jane said, and I might have detected a touch of envy in her voice. "Jackie, you're just full of surprises. Why didn't you tell us?"

"I'm telling you now. And, besides, they only just asked me last week."

"What's the column going to be called?" Plain Jane asked. That was a question I wouldn't have even thought to ask but, after all, Plain Jane had written for some of the big-name magazines in New York.

"Chatter Box."

"Chatter Box?"

"Meaning little bits of news and delightful gossip," Jackie said. "And my byline will be Miss Dreamsville." After a pause, she said, "The owner came up with the Chatter Box thing. I'm not sure I like it, either. But I won the more important battle. It will *not* be on the Women's Page! It will be on the Editorial Page."

"What's wrong with the Women's Page?"

Mrs. Bailey White asked innocently.

"No, no, no, I will never write for the Women's Page," Jackie said crossly. "It's all weddings and gardening tips and all that junk. No, no, no! I don't want my column to be stuck there!"

"But everyone reads the Women's Page," Mrs. Bailey White said softly.

"Men don't!" Jackie cried out. "If it's on the Women's Page it implies that my column is for women only or about women's 'concerns' and that's not what I'm going to write about."

"Well, what are you going to write about?" asked Plain Jane.

Jackie smiled, and to me it seemed a little mischievous. "The agreement is that I get to write my column about anything I want. My first column is supposed to run in two days and I couldn't decide what to write about. The editor suggested a piece about how Collier County seems to be forgotten at the statehouse in Tallahassee. But that seems deadly dull, doesn't it? Now I'm thinking I could write about Seminole Joe."

"What?" I asked, realizing I was at least one step behind Jackie's thinking.

"Well, what if I wrote a piece about Seminole Joe, pointing out that he haunts the area where Darryl is going to do all that

123

construction? And maybe get everyone in Naples all scared and stirred up, so there'd be opposition to the project?"

This was either the best or worst idea I ever heard. I'd have to think on it overnight to decide which. In some respects it was brilliant. It might even work. On the other hand, it was one of those ideas that could have consequences we couldn't anticipate. Jackie had a history of getting herself, and everyone else around her, in over their head. She was good at coming up with creative ideas but her strong suit didn't include fixing up the messes that sometimes resulted.

She saw our hesitation. "Aw come on, girls! What could go wrong?"

Not the words I wanted to hear, but I admired her confidence just the same.

TWELVE

If he hadn't been so overburdened with work, Ted Hart might have enjoyed the challenge to start an airline for Mr. Toomb, his boss. The fact was that he was already away from his wife and kids more than he or they had expected. Hopefully, Mr. Toomb would quickly allow him to hire an assistant.

But he was off to a bad start. He and Mr. Toomb could not even agree on a name for the airline. Ted had suggested Florida Airlines. Mr. Toomb's idea? Wild Blue Yonder Airways. Ted could see immediately that marketing would be a problem. The word "wild" could be interpreted as "reckless." And "yonder" had a connotation that was anything but sophisticated. The well-heeled Yankees they would need as customers were not going to like it. Well, Mr. Toomb was the boss, and the boss always got what he wanted. Especially if the boss was a powerful, no-nonsense man like Mr. Toomb.

Ted spent two weeks in Tallahassee to get the permits lined up. It was easy compared to the way things were done up north, Ted thought. In fact, before anyone realized what was happening, the crummy little airport landing strip in Naples was under construction. The Naples airport had been so lacking that Mr. Toomb had been forced to accept that headquarters for his new airline would be in Tampa, which was, compared to Naples, an actual city. Meanwhile, the headline in the Naples paper said the state was financing some "improvements" to the humble airstrip, but in truth it was being modernized and expanded to accommodate Mr. Toomb's vision.

One problem was going to be Ted's son, Judd, who was deeply involved with the cadet corps of the Civil Air Patrol. Making a mental note to himself, Ted vowed to be careful not to say too much around Judd, who seemed to be on friendly terms with everyone at the Naples Airport. Mr. Toomb was a secretive man, which meant Ted — if he wanted to stay employed — had to keep secrets, too. Not that Mr. Toomb was doing anything illegal, Ted quickly told himself. Mr. Toomb was an opportunist. A well-connected opportunist, the most formidable kind.

Ted sighed. This was not what he thought he was getting into, back when he was in the Army during the war and wanted to make the world a better place. Somehow that dream had been diverted, one little decision at a time, into a simpler, more *personal* goal: go to college on the G.I. Bill and become the first person in his family to wear a suit to work. It had meant leaving Boston, which he hadn't counted on. It had meant long days on the road, travel, and, needless to say, time away from Jackie and the kids. Was it worth it? On good days, the answer was yes.

Jackie's parents, owners of a well-known restaurant in downtown Boston, were not happy when Ted proposed to their only daughter. Sometimes it occurred to him that he was still trying to prove himself to them, even though he knew it could never happen. They would not even come to visit. It wasn't Florida they were opposed to; God knows they'd spent their fair share of time at the Fontainebleau in Miami Beach and the Breakers in Palm Beach. They just wouldn't come to Collier County, that's all. In their minds, Collier County was the sticks.

Of course, the way things were headed, his in-laws might change their stubborn minds about Naples. There could come a time when Naples *surpassed* the swankier places on Florida's east coast. Not likely, but possible.

As for his own parents, they didn't have the money to travel to Cape Cod for a holiday, let alone Naples. In fact he wasn't sure if his parents had ever gone on a vacation. This thought made him so sad that he found it necessary to light his pipe, a habit that calmed him.

He watched as a tiny, single-engine plane landed gracefully on the lone runway and taxied carefully around construction equipment and scores of workmen who hadn't even looked up when it landed. There were no hangars, only the terminal building which housed a weather station, a bathroom, and a so-called lobby with a half-dozen molded plastic chairs, a Coke machine, and plenty of ashtrays. He'd seen better accommodations overseas in the Army during World War Two.

He had no desire to feel nostalgic about his stint in the Army. Back in Boston, he'd had a few beers now and then at a local VFW but, unlike many other veterans, he discovered he couldn't think of his war service as his glory days. Unusual for his generation, Ted was bitter about the war. About all wars. About powerful old men, since the beginning of time, who sent young men to their deaths. More than nine thousand Allied soldiers killed or injured on D-Day alone. Ted thought about those numbers every day.

He watched another plane land then realized that his pipe had grown cold. He leaned over to empty the bowl by tapping it against the heel of his shoe and was surprised, a moment later, to realize that he'd struck the pipe so hard that he'd broken it in two. He was glad no one was around to see this. Men like him didn't show their emotions when it came to the war.

His unit had landed at Normandy without him. He had been pulled out at the last minute and never knew why. The shame and guilt resulted in unrelenting pressure. *You should have been there,* his mind told him daily. *You'd better have a good life; you're living for all of those who didn't make it.*

Twenty years had passed but it didn't matter. And, as luck would have it, there were fresh reminders. The only suitable type of aircraft available for Mr. Toomb's airline, it turned out, were old Army transport planes affectionately known as "Gooney Birds."

And the pilots? The only ones who had answered the newspaper advertisements were former World War Two pilots who had kept up their credentials in civilian life. He'd already hired two.

So far, the federal government had approved a route between Tampa and points east (Orlando) and north (Tallahassee). It was a huge accomplishment in a short period of time, but much work remained to be done. When he was younger and dreamed of the white-collar life, Ted had envisioned smoke-filled boardrooms and leisurely lunches of prime rib and bourbon. In his mind, a secretary would take care of all the mundane details at work, just as a wife would do at home. Well, fantasy did not match reality. While he was making more money than he'd ever thought possible, the truth was that he hardly had time to enjoy spending it.

At least Jackie seemed happy now. Their first year in Florida had been tumultuous. Between the book club and the radio show, she'd caused quite a ruckus. She had irritated the heck out of Mr. Toomb, but even that seemed smoothed over. The book club had mostly disbanded, and Jackie was spending most of her time helping with that baby. Yes, it was a bit unorthodox, but it was certainly worthwhile. He was relieved by the decision by Jackie and her friends to keep the baby primarily at Mrs. Bailey White's house, which was off the beaten path. It also meant that the baby's mother, Priscilla, could stay there — and not at his house — when she returned on her visits from college. Ted was not prejudiced, or at least he didn't think he was. However, a man had to protect his wife and children, and he was not going to let them be a target for some furious redneck who might throw a Molotov cocktail through the living room window.

Like Jackie, he believed that the best way to address the race problem in America was to help Negroes advance through education. In fact, one of Ted's favorite charities was the United Negro College Fund, to which he donated every year since it was founded in 1944, even when his wallet had been thin. He had met Priscilla only once, but he agreed with Jackie that the young girl was college material.

He was surprised — but kept it to himself — that Jackie seemed to be enjoying the baby as much as she did. He recalled how brittle she had been as a new mother and it was interesting to see that she was so relaxed with Priscilla's baby. Maybe, because Jackie was a little older now, and experienced. Jackie's friend, Plain Jane, seemed to be enjoying the baby, too, at least judging from Jackie's comments. He had his doubts about weird old Mrs. Bailey White, but from everything he'd heard, the old woman had paid her debt to society and was settling back into a normal life. If Jackie and Plain Jane were, in a sense, helping with Mrs. Bailey White's rehabilitation, that seemed like a good cause, too.

Obviously, this was not the life Jackie expected when she'd married him. Of course, it wasn't what he had planned on, either. If only there'd been a way to climb the corporate ladder without being on the road so much of the time, or relocating the whole family to a place that seemed as far from Boston as Timbuktu.

THIRTEEN

Dolores Simpson did not have a radio or television, nor did she care to. Even if owning one or both had been her heart's desire, the electric grid didn't come anywhere near her little fishing shack. She had considered buying one of those newfangled transistor radios, but it cost too much. As for a telephone, the thought was laughable. It would be "a hundred years shy of never," as the saying went, before anyone put phone lines there.

Robbie-Lee had been her grapevine to the outside world. He would come home from school — and later, from his job at Sears — and tell her the big news of the day (the Cuban Missile Crisis, for example) along with local news (who had gotten married, who had up and died) and, best of all, little tidbits from Hollywood that he heard on the radio during his lunch hour. If he had something new to tell her about Elizabeth

Taylor, it made her day.

But those days were gone. She didn't miss people in general. She just missed Robbie-Lee. And with changes coming to the river, she needed the information that her son, had he still been living at home, would have provided. Walking to town was tiring, but she'd done it when necessary, for example, when she'd sent the telegram to Dora Witherspoon in Mississippi. Fortunately, her neighbors, Billy and Marco, aware that Robbie-Lee had gone away, had started dropping off the *Naples Star* at her fishing shack on their way back from — well, from somewhere. She never really knew what they were up to but followed the unofficial rule of Gun Rack Village: Don't ask questions.

The gift of a newspaper miraculously landing on her narrow dock, courtesy of Billy and Marco, didn't occur every day but it was often enough to suit her. She no longer had to keep track of the passage of days by marking a scrap of paper each morning. She didn't care that the newspaper was secondhand; there were signs, like cigarette ashes smudged into the newsprint, that the brothers had read it already. That was fine; it meant she didn't have to pay them.

On this particular day Dolores heard the truck followed by the familiar *thump* as the paper hit the dock but didn't bother to retrieve it right away. Not a thing was happening of any importance. For real news — news that mattered — she'd have to wait for Dora Witherspoon.

Only when she went outside an hour later to clean her shotgun did she remember the newspaper, saw it sitting there, and picked it up. She took the rubber band off (she saved them; they were hard to come by) and saw this announcement on the front page:

"Read Our New Column by Collier
County's Very Own MISS
DREAMSVILLE!" page 11

Like everyone else in Naples, Dolores flipped immediately to page eleven. Peering out at her was a little pen-and-ink sketch of a grinning, winking woman who was clearly supposed to be Jackie. Next to the drawing were the words "Chatter Box by Miss Dreamsville!"

There was a headline beneath it that read, THE LEGEND OF SEMINOLE JOE. Dolores did not take the time to sit down or go back in the house. She read it standing stock still, not even bothered by a sliver of sunlight

135

breaking through some bad-weather clouds and shining in her eyes. Some of the words were hard for her so she read slowly and aloud:

Residents have long spoken in hushed tones about a dangerous apparition who is said to reside near the Mangrove River and has been known to wreak havoc in our lovely community.

Seminole Joe, as he is called, has killed (and, some say, eaten) at least seventeen persons since he himself was murdered by Spanish Explorers. It is believed he only attacks Caucasian men. Mr. Joe has been fairly quiet in recent years, but old-timers are concerned this will change with the proposed new real-estate development (cheekily called Dreamsville Estates by Mr. Darryl Norwood, who, it should be stated here, did not ask permission of yours truly).

Since the beginning of time, one of the peculiarities of the human condition is that people can look at the exact same event, or in this case, the same place, and see entirely different things. Some look at the river and see Nature in all her glory. Others envision a river of money, created with asphalt, timber, and glass. It is not hard to imagine which side Seminole Joe will take as it is widely known that he abhors change and wanton waste.

A model citizen who has lived in Collier County for all of her eighty years was willing to speak but not for attribution. "I'm very worried that Joe will get all stirred up again," she remarked. "Anyone working on that project, or living there after it's built, will never again have a sound night's sleep. I know I won't."

Will Neapolitans be safe from the wrath of the ghostly Indian? Will Seminole Joe rise again? Only time will tell.

Dolores crumpled the newspaper in her hands and tossed it as far as she could, only to have a wind gust pick it up and toss it straight back, mocking her. What was that crazy Boston gal up to now? Having her involved was not helpful. The woman made a mess of everything she touched. Why was she bringing up *Seminole Joe*?

Old-timers knew it wasn't wise to talk about Seminole Joe unless you absolutely had to, and then, only in quiet, funeral-parlor voices. You surely didn't write about him in the newspaper.

The fact that Darryl was planning to call his development Dreamsville Estates was a shock. A wickedly clever business idea on

137

Darryl's part. But what kind of fool would provoke Jackie Hart and Seminole Joe at the same time?

Over the years, Dolores had occasionally heard a child being disciplined by a thoughtless parent saying, "You'd better behave or Seminole Joe will get you tonight." Well, first of all, Dolores thought that was mean. Why would anyone scare a child like that? She'd never talked to Robbie-Lee like that. Second, Seminole Joe wouldn't be bothered with some poor skeerty-cat child who hadn't done his homework or his chores. He had far more worthwhile wrongs to right. Besides, no one could summon Seminole Joe for selfish reasons. Some spirits could be conjured for specific reasons, but not Joe. He had a mind of his own.

Jackie was the type of Yankee who, no doubt, would laugh at the idea of Seminole Joe, like the woman manager who came down from Chicago to train Robbie-Lee to run the Sears catalog store. Miss High and Mighty had interrupted a conversation between Robbie-Lee and a customer by announcing, "What are you talking about?! Surely you know there is no such thing as ghosts!" And, according to Robbie-Lee, it was said in a way that made both him and the customer feel ignorant.

Dolores knew the type. What the lady manager didn't say, but might as well have, was, "I don't believe in them, therefore, they cannot possibly exist." Dolores knew differently. The truth was, if you didn't encounter spirits it was because you refused to see them — possibly, to your own detriment.

Why were Yankees so certain they understood the world better than anyone else? You'd think life was some kind of big joke, and they were the only ones smart enough to know what was funny and what was not. Folks like that weren't open to mystery or magic. They thought they had everything figured out, so their minds were closed like a steel trap. It was kind of sad, when you got right down to it.

Maybe the problem was that Yankee folks, even on vacation, were always in motion, running from one activity to the next. If they weren't swimming, they were golfing. If they weren't golfing, they were boating. That was fine — they were welcome to it — but Dolores was puzzled that people could claim to love the outdoor life and yet seem so far away from nature. They preferred houses built like bunkers with cement floors and walls, barriers to the swampland where, God forbid, bugs and other scary things lurked. Dolores imagined them in their nice houses, some with air-conditioning, all of them with plumbing. They put on shoes that looked like combat boots, just to walk to their mailboxes. She'd seen them and tried not to laugh.

Did they ever spend hours looking at the stars, as Dolores did? There was nothing quite like star watching on a clear night, or witnessing the fight for survival among the plants and critters in the swamps, to make a person remember that she was just a speck of dust.

Seminole Joe was more than a story. He was a spirit, and spirits live on, in different ways and for different reasons.

What most folks didn't seem to understand was that Seminole Joe was the spirit of injustice. He represented all the wrongs that had been done in the 'Glades. Folks were scared of Seminole Joe but in her opinion, it was Darryl they should have been skeert of. Darryl was like an overseer with a whip, a man with no soul. Darryl was a man who had choices, and he'd chosen mean over good.

From time to time, Dolores actually understood — just a little — what it must have been like to be colored or Indian. It didn't take a genius to see that white people were at the root of just about every mess you could think of, and Darryl was just the latest version. White folks had a knack for finding their way to the top of the pecking order and ruling the roost. Dolores could see this, and yet it created a problem for her because she was white, so what was wrong with her? What was she lacking? Why wasn't she rich and powerful, and sitting at the top of the henhouse looking down on everyone else? Maybe she wasn't quite mean enough. Or ambitious enough.

She uncrumpled the newspaper and re-read the column. Jackie Hart's bringing up Seminole Joe was bound to complicate an already-tricky situation. Jackie seemed to thrive when she created chaos. But Dolores had lived long enough to know that a wise person didn't let a bobcat out of its cage and assume it would eat only varmints. No, sir, it might eat you instead.

She looked over at the night heron. "Let's hope Dora Witherspoon talks some sense into her man," she called out, and the bird stretched its wings in response. To herself, she added, "Otherwise, I'm afeared we be in for a wild ride."

FOURTEEN

"What do you suppose Seminole Joe looks like?" Judd asked, wiping the sweat from his brow with the hem of his T-shirt. He had fled to my little cottage to get away from the craziness that had been going on all day, ever since the *Naples Star* landed in people's driveways or hedges. Judd said the phone had not stopped ringing with excited people wanting to talk to his mother about her column on Seminole Joe. No wonder he wanted to hide out for a while at my cottage. And I put him to work, helping me dig some new holes for the turtles to wallow around in.

"Haven't you ever seen the local Indians?" I asked, surprised.

"You mean selling baskets?" he said. "No one ever said they were Indians. I didn't know who they were. My teacher said we should stay away from them, that's all I know."

"Well, did you ever see the movie *Key Largo*?" I asked.

He looked like he was racking his brain. "No, I don't think so," he said. "That was before my time."

Judd cracked me up. Sometimes he sounded like a thirteen-year-old boy, and sometimes he sounded like a sixty-year-old man.

"Well," I said, slurping on my iced tea, "Lauren Bacall was in it. And Humphrey Bogart."

"Seminole Joe looks like . . . Humphrey Bogart?"

I tried not to laugh. "No, no, Humphrey Bogart plays a man who was in the Army in the war and visits his dead friend's father and widow who live down yon in Key Largo. There's a bunch of gangsters in the movie, too — Edward G. Robinson plays one of them."

The word "gangster" got Judd's attention. He was behaving like a thirteen-year-old again. "So what happens?" he said, completely focused. I noticed, once again, that he had Jackie's blue eyes — the exact shade. And yet he looked like his dad, Ted Hart, too.

"Well, the real star of the movie is a storm," I said. "A hurricane. But maybe I shouldn't tell you more. Sometime maybe you'll see the movie and I wouldn't want to ruin it for you."

"But — wait — what's this got to do with Seminole Joe?"

"There are characters in the movie who are supposed to be Seminole Indians," I said, "and I think some of them really are. So Joe probably looked more or less like the Indians in *Key Largo.*"

Judd looked disappointed. "But how am I going to see the movie?" he said. "It could be five years before they show it on TV."

"You could go to the library and see if they have any books on the Seminoles," I said, and his face brightened. "They must at least have a book about Andrew Jackson and the Seminole Wars," I added.

Well, that was the last I saw of Judd that day. He was off on his bicycle like Paul Revere warning folks that the British were coming, an image that fit mighty nice, considering that he'd spent the first eleven years of his life in Boston.

Judd's energy was inspiring. After fixing myself a fried bologna sandwich, half of which I fed to my turtles, I decided to go for a stroll on the beach to look for shells and clear my mind. To my surprise, every little shell or pebble seemed to hurt my bare feet. In my year away from home, it seems I'd become a tenderfoot on account of wearing shoes all the time. But the surf was gentle and soothing as bathwater, and I realized, splashing along in ankle-deep water, that I was happy. Not happy about Darryl's development plans or his remarriage to some Northern gal, of course, but happy with the general direction of my life. I had learned a great deal during my year in Mississippi — some of it hard to take — but I was more independent than I'd ever been. I was going back to Jackson, not forever, but for a little while longer. I was not going to run away from the city of my mother's birth and the story that was unfolding there about her past. *My* past.

There was still plenty of daylight, so I went home, found my old Keds, and walked slowly downtown. I told myself I was going to get a root beer float at the Rexall counter but truth be told, I wanted to see if anything was going on. Sometimes, folks would gather downtown when something important was happening. I'd be able to judge how big a reaction Jackie's story was getting by the number of people — usually at home on a hot night in Naples — milling around and looking for an excuse to talk.

Sure enough, there were people gathered

by the bench in front of the post office, outside the Rexall, and by the Winn-Dixie. I recognized a few people from high school but wasn't eager to talk to them, especially Betty Jane Pomeroy, who was holding court over by the Green Stamp Redemption Center. Betty Jane had a way of inserting the topic of her happy marriage, brilliant children, and fabulous house into every conversation. Fortunately, I saw Plain Jane walking along by herself from the direction of the Dairy Queen. We saw each other at the same moment, and I was reminded, once again, how much my old book club meant to me. Before them, especially since I'd gotten divorced, I'd felt like a stranger in my own hometown.

Plain Jane and I perched on the top step of the Everglades Savings and Loan, a good location for spying on people ever since it was rebuilt at eight feet above sea level after being trounced by Hurricane Donna. "You know what they're talking about, don't you?" Plain Jane said, between bites of an ice cream cone that was melting faster than she could eat it.

"I can guess," I said.

"Someone said Darryl is going to have a press conference tomorrow," she said. "Apparently she really stirred things up. You know, people don't talk about spirits, much less Seminole Joe. Everyone around here knows the stories but no one has ever written about it in the newspaper."

This was true. Somehow, just the fact that Seminole Joe had made the pages of the *Naples Star* made a scary story seem real. Official. Or, as Mama would have said, bona fide.

Hard to say where this was headed, though. Were they upset about Seminole Joe, or mad at Jackie for writing about him? Would their fear become anger at Darryl for possibly disturbing Seminole Joe?

That night I didn't sleep well and I bet the same was true for half the population of Collier County. I couldn't decide which was worse: to sleep with the windows shut and die of the heat or leave them open and possibly be ax-murdered by Seminole Joe. When I finally fell asleep, my eyes were closed but my ears were wide open, and any little sound had me leaping out of the bed.

The next day, the *Naples Star* carried this story on the front page:

STRONG RESPONSE TO
'MISS DREAMSVILLE' DEBUT
by the Editors
Collier County residents reacted with

unusual animosity yesterday to an opinion piece by our new columnist, Mrs. Jackie Hart, also known as Miss Dreamsville, after her famous radio show of that name. Our phone rang off the hook yesterday from calls by readers incensed by Miss Dreamsville's (and this newspaper's) decision to publish an account of the legend of Seminole Joe. A logbook kept by our staff showed that eighty-seven callers complained that Seminole Joe did not like attention and that Miss Dreamsville's column could cause him to rise from his ghostly grave and commit new atrocities. We find this highly unlikely, although we are flattered that so many residents assume that Seminole Joe is a faithful reader of the *Naples Star.* Collier County residents, let us remember that "Joe" is a legend! This is 1964, the Modern Age, and as such it is time we put these superstitions to rest, or at least keep them in check, or our fine community will remain stuck in the putrid fog of backward thinking. We will be running a special Letters to the Editor section on Friday to address readers' concerns. In a related development, Mr. Darryl Norwood has announced that he will hold a press conference today at 7:00 PM to answer questions about his project.

Well, I had the answer to my question. So far, at least, people were more upset with Jackie and the newspaper than they were with Darryl. As I tried to decide what to do next, Judd came by on his bicycle. He said he'd tried to call his father, who was in Tallahassee, but hadn't been able to reach him.

"Mom was on the phone with a lawyer in New York City, then she got so mad she left the house," he confided. "I tried to call Dad but the long-distance operator wouldn't make the call because I'm a kid."

Judd left, but not before agreeing to go with me to the press conference in case Jackie showed up and made a scene. I would rather have a tooth pulled without novocaine but I knew in my heart I had to go — for Judd's sake, at least.

About two o'clock in the afternoon, while I was writing a letter to Mrs. Conroy, my landlady back in Mississippi, I heard Jackie's car pull up. To my surprise, she marched right in — right past Norma Jean, Myrtle, and Castro. This was not a good sign. She was so mad she forgot to be afraid of "those dreadful things."

"That odious, reprehensible, son of a lobster boat!" she hollered, by way of a greeting. I'd never heard anyone utter that particular string of words before but, considering the circumstances, I figured this was some kind of exotic, Northern insult. I was relieved somewhat by the realization that I was not likely the intended recipient of her anger.

She remained in the doorway, her hand still on the knob of my front door, and yelled again. "He's going to get away with it! He can *use my name*!"

"Jackie," I said, my voice shaking, "come sit down." I approached her gingerly, like she was a wild critter that had escaped from Jungle Larry's African Safari, a tourist trap on the Tamiami Trail. Carefully, I took her arm and led her to Mama's old chair, where she collapsed in a theatrical heap. I left her side long enough to retrieve a tall glass of sweet tea and carry it back to her on a little tray with a napkin. After a few sips, she was calm enough to tell me what had happened. She spoke in short, little sentences, like she was going to blow a fuse if she tried to say a whole sentence at once.

"I talked to the lawyer. On the phone. I called him long distance."

I waited. "Well," I said. "What did he say?"

She swallowed hard. "Darryl can call his development Dreamsville if he wants. He just can't use my picture on any of the advertisements. He can't say that I endorsed

150

it, since that would be a lie. But he doesn't have to get my permission to call it Dreamsville, or Dreamsville Estates."

"I see." Actually, I didn't understand it at all.

"I don't 'own' the name Miss Dreamsville," she added, sensing my confusion. "Not in a legal sense."

"So you can't sue him?" I asked quietly.

"Well, I could sue him. But I wouldn't win."

"And that's what the lawyer told you? On the phone?"

Jackie lit a cigarette. "Yes," she said. "That's the way it is. Unfortunately."

"And this was the lawyer in New York?"

"I called two — one in New York, the other in Boston. They both said the same thing."

I let this sink in. Jackie seemed more relaxed, like she'd used up all her anger, but I was becoming madder by the second. What the heck was wrong with Darryl that he would steal my friend's name? Was this another swipe at me? I had to admit it was, in a sickening way, an ingenious move on his part. Jackie had put Naples on the map with her radio show. Even Walter Cronkite, the most trusted man in America, had done a little segment on *CBS Evening News* about

151

Miss Dreamsville. It would be easy for Darryl to market his new development to Yankees by calling it Dreamsville Estates.

I hoped Mama wasn't listening in on my thoughts. She never had approved of cussin' in any way, shape, or form. But all I could think of was, *That odious, reprehensible, son of a lobster boat.*

Fifteen

The challenge at the press conference would be keeping Jackie from speaking her mind. Judd and I made her promise six ways to Sunday that she wouldn't say a single word, what with her talent for making bad things worse.

"Jackie, tonight we are going to be flies on the wall," I kept admonishing her as we walked downtown from my cottage.

"Yes, all we're going to do is collect intelligence," Judd added.

"Judd Hart, you've been watching too much of that spy stuff on television," Jackie scolded.

"Mom, what I'm saying is that we should lay low and observe what happens. Then we can reconvene and plan our next move."

Jackie sighed and ruffled Judd's hair. "Do you think the girls will show up?" she asked, referring to her twin daughters — Judd's older sisters.

"Not a chance," Judd said.

"Well, that's good because I wouldn't want to embarrass them," Jackie said. "They think I'm *embarrassing enough* already."

"They're girls, Mom," Judd said soothingly. "They're weird."

Jackie looked at Judd as if she were going to say something more but didn't. Instead, she ruffled his hair again.

"You're not going to embarrass anyone," I said firmly, trying to get back to the point. "You will be dignified, like Elizabeth Taylor in *Cleopatra.*"

Jackie had insisted we go early and stand directly in front of the stage set up by the Chamber of Commerce on the grass next to City Hall. I would rather we stood in back but I soon realized what she hoped to accomplish. She wanted everyone to see her. She stood with her arms crossed, staring tragically into the distance. Judd put one hand on her shoulder protectively. I copied Jackie's stance except I planned to look eyeball-to-eyeball with Darryl once he started speaking.

Just as I began to think everyone was staying home, folks starting showing up in little groups of two and three. By the time the press conference started, five minutes late, there were close to two hundred people there, all itching to hear what Darryl had to say. Of course, this being a small Southern town, we had to be patient. First, the mayor led us in the Pledge of Allegiance followed by the Sons of the Confederate Veterans performance of "Dixie." After that, Little Miss Swamp Buggy 1964 sang "Collier County, I Love Thee" and a rousing rendition of "Yay! Rah! for Naples."

Yay! Rah! for Naples,
Yay! Rah! for Naples,
Someone in the crowd's singing,
"Yay! Rah! for Naples."
One, two, three, four,
Naples, that's us! Rah, rah, rah . . .

And then came a string of announcements: The Garden Club needed volunteers to water the flower boxes near the train station (even though most people arrived by car or bus and hardly any trains came through anymore). And someone from the Naples Players announced that the new season would start the following week with *Stop the World — I Want to Get Off,* starring Bucky Holmes from the Esso station.

By the time Darryl was about to speak, I had the embarrassing image of myself crumpling to the ground and being placed on a cot and resuscitated by the eager Boy Scouts who were manning the first-aid squad. Judd looked flushed and Jackie, a bit glassy-eyed, was having trouble maintaining her pose.

The mayor spoke briefly. "I'm sure we all know Darryl Norwood, who grew up right here in Collier County, and is making it his personal goal to bring us into a new era." I was relieved to hear grumbles in the crowd, and there was no applause when Darryl took the microphone.

"I know why you all are here, and I'm grateful for it," he began. "I'm glad for the opportunity to straighten out any misunderstandings. It's very important that you all understand that Dreamsville Estates will be the best thing that ever happened to Collier County. And I want to assure all of you that all of this needless fear about Seminole Joe is not helpful. Frankly, I'm surprised that in this day and age, y'all would get yourselves worked up into a lather over the idea that we could be disturbing a haint." He paused, and laughed dismissively. "There is no such thing as Seminole Joe. There never was."

I had to hide a grin that was creeping up the corners of my mouth. Darryl was handling this all wrong. I knew it before he did; I could feel it in the crowd.

An old-timer with skin like cowhide elbowed his way to the front and struggled up to the platform. "Don't you go talking down to us," he shouted into the microphone. "We gonna believe what we want to believe. You're a dog-gone fool. You're playing games with the devil and we aren't going to allow it!"

The crowd cheered like their team had just scored a touchdown against Punta Gorda High. Clearly, Darryl was losing. If everyone continued on this path, the people of Naples were turning their anger from Jackie and the newspaper to Darryl, where it belonged.

I peeked at Jackie and could see she was biting her lower lip. Poor gal, it was killin' her not to get into the fray.

Just when it seemed the sheriff might need to tell everyone to settle down, the mayor stood up and prevailed upon us to behave in a more Christian manner. "We are civilized people," he scolded, holding the microphone so close that it screeched and hurt our ears. "Sorry about that," he said. Then, "We must remain calm and listen to our speaker. These are the leaders of our community, and we should be respectful."

"Darryl Norwood ain't a leader!" a youthful voice called from deep within the crowd.

"We never elected him to nothin'!"

The Reverend Wesley Whitmore from Sweet Savior Baptist Church took the microphone from the mayor, who didn't look at all sorry and retreated quickly to the back of the stage. "I have something I would like to say," the reverend said in a voice deep as a bullfrog's in mating season. "Talking about haints and conjuring and black magic and whatnot is not worthy of this community." He received a polite round of applause mostly, I noticed, from his parishioners.

Darryl tried to take advantage of the preacher's comments. "Thank you," he said, leaning into the microphone, still in the clutches of the preacher. "Y'all should listen to Reverend Whitmore here."

But the good reverend snapped back. "Now just a moment," he said to Darryl, "don't presume to pretend that I'm endorsing your project. I'm just saying that folks should stop this nonsense about . . . well, about an Indian spirit. And another thing," he added, "I don't think it's nice that you're planning to call the place Dreamsville Estates when Mrs. Jackie Hart doesn't approve. She's our Miss Dreamsville, and it's disrespectful to use a lady's name against her wishes, and to profit from it."

This was a surprise. Of course, Reverend Whitmore was new here. He'd never heard Jackie's at-times risqué radio show and had missed the uproar she had caused.

Defending a lady's good name was a surefire way to stir up a crowd anywhere south of the Mason-Dixon line, and it most definitely had that effect in good old Naples. The crowd applauded warmly. Jackie, seizing the moment, waved and mouthed, "Thank you."

Then another preacher stood up and the Reverend Whitmore handed over the microphone. "My name is Reverend John McDaniel," he said politely, "and I'm the new interim pastor at Airport Road Methodist. I am from North Florida and I was educated in Chicago. I am in full agreement with Reverend Whitmore here, but I'd like to add something else, if I may. Last month, as I traveled nearly the length of our great state with my family to arrive here at my new appointment, I was alarmed at the pace of development in so many places. Why is this? I asked myself. Is it *progress,* as some would say, or is it worship of that false God, *money*? And, what are the consequences? These undeveloped areas are a gift from God, my friends. Remember your scripture — we are *stewards* of God's earth."

The mayor jumped up from his seat and grabbed the microphone a little roughly from Reverend McDaniel. "Now let's get back on track here," he said. "This project is a mighty good thing for Naples. Dreamsville Estates will attract people from all over the United States. The Chamber of Commerce has already agreed to sponsor Welcome to Dreamsville signs at every entrance to Naples. Our airport needs work, and we are fortunate that one of our most eminent citizens, Mr. Toomb, has agreed to oversee some improvements there. Neapolitans, we must think of the big picture! We already have two major assets — the fishing pier and the swamp buggy races. Three of the world's great religions — Baptists, Methodists, and Presbyterians — are represented right here in our little town. We are a welcoming place and it's about time we move forward into the nineteenth century."

"What? Don't you mean twentieth century?" someone hollered from the back of the crowd, which exploded into laughter, the kind with a mean edge to it. Emboldened, the heckler added, "Just what century do you think we be livin' in, Mayor? I thought this was 1964. Are you saying this is 1864?"

The mayor looked upset and ruffled like a

hen that's being bothered by a rooster. "Aw, heck, you know what I mean!" he said. Now that even the mayor had been set back on his heels, it was fair to say that Jackie, the *Naples Star,* and Seminole Joe had won the day, with Darryl the loser. So far, so good.

Judd took off for civil Air Patrol, and Jackie and I, feeling a little triumphant, went to Mrs. Bailey White's house. Our good mood soured immediately, though, because, of all things, Mrs. Bailey White was peeved that Jackie had mentioned her in the newspaper column. Jackie admitted that the line about the "model citizen who has lived in Collier County for all of her eighty years" and who feared the return of Seminole Joe was indeed a reference to Mrs. Bailey White. What I didn't get — and I could see that Jackie was puzzled, too — was that Mrs. Bailey White's name had not even been mentioned.

"I do not like the whole world thinking of me as eighty years old," she said, brushing a piece of lint off her skirt.

"But no one will know it's you," Jackie said, trying to sound reassuring.

"Well, I know it's me, and that's enough," Mrs. Bailey White sulked. "A woman should never reveal her true age. Do you know what they say about a woman who will reveal her age? That she'll reveal everything else, too! And I wasn't raised like that."

Plain Jane, who had been reading the final pages of *To the Lighthouse,* set down her book. "Mrs. Bailey White, I don't see why —"

"And I'll tell you something else," Mrs. Bailey White interrupted. "A woman should only be in the paper two times in her life — when she gets married and when she dies."

"But Mrs. Bailey White," I started but stopped short. What I wanted to say was, *But you must have been in the newspapers plenty of times when you were arrested, tried, and convicted for shooting your husband back in the day.*

"Please believe me, Mrs. Bailey White, I am very, very sorry," Jackie said, as I prayed silently for an end to this uncomfortable conversation. "It was stupid of me. I should have thought of it. And it won't happen again."

"Well," Mrs. Bailey White said slowly, "I guess maybe it doesn't matter. Maybe I'm being too thin-skinned. All this talk about Seminole Joe is getting on my last good nerve. And, yes, I know it's my fault because I'm the one who brought him up —"

"Oh, no," Jackie said quickly. "This is my fault."

"No, it's not," I said, wondering why women were always quick to blame ourselves. "It's that no-good, good-for-nothin' former husband of mine. That's whose fault it is. He started all this mess and everyone's in an uproar because of it. And you know what? The louse is getting married again."

There were sighs and groans enough to fill a graveyard on Halloween. "Oh, Dora," Plain Jane said, speaking for the rest. "That's too bad. Or, at least I think it must be . . . Oh dear, how do you feel about it?"

"Not great, especially because she's a Northern gal," I said miserably.

"Why does that make you feel worse?" Jackie asked.

"Oh, I don't know. Maybe because I just assume she must be smarter and prettier than me," I said.

"She's probably meaner than a wet hen," Mrs. Bailey White said. "Where's she from?"

"Some town in New Jersey called Basking Ridge. That's what Darryl said."

"Oh!" Jackie said. We looked at her in alarm. "Basking Ridge — that's the place where Darryl's investors live! That's what Ted said."

We were puzzling through the implications

of this until Plain Jane finally put it into words. "So maybe Darryl is marrying into the family that is paying for his real estate development?" she said aloud.

That was a disgusting thought. The possibility of Darryl marrying for money could mean he was even more of a low-level creep than I thought.

I hadn't even thought of bringing up the topic of Darryl and his remarriage but I was glad that I had. Sharing my distress about Darryl's remarriage reminded me that I loved my friends. I *needed* my friends. And, despite the depressing reason for my return, at this moment I was thrilled to be back. I was still a member of the Collier County Women's Literary Society, and it felt awfully good.

Sixteen

The airline business was far more complex than Ted Hart had anticipated. First of all, there were the unions, the most obstinate being the pilots' organization which made it difficult for Ted to create schedules that made any kind of sense from a financial point of view. Then there was the government (pronounced *guv-mint* up in Tallahassee, Ted's new home away from home). The state didn't have many regulations when it came to commercial airlines but at the federal level, administrators kept close tabs.

To Ted it seemed like interference until one of the pilots, who had flown so many missions during the war that it was a miracle he survived, gave him a wake-up call on the tarmac in Orlando. "All you talk about is profit margin! What do you want us to do, kill the passengers?" the pilot yelled. And for a moment, Ted thought he was about to get shoved straight into a propeller of a

DC-3. Afterward, he realized the pilot had been right. He — Ted Hart, a blue-collar son of Fall River, Massachusetts — had put money ahead of people. It was one of the worst moments of his life.

He walked away from the runway and lit his new pipe, which he'd purchased after breaking the old one. He hadn't been able to give up smoking but at least he quit a cigarette habit. If only Jackie would do the same. The woman smoked like a chimney. The kids complained about it all the time. The Surgeon General's announcement earlier that year about a strong link between cigarettes and cancer had an impact on him, but not Jackie.

Maybe, Ted thought, he should throw in the towel. All he really wanted was to go home, not that Naples was "home," exactly, but that's where Jackie and the kids were living and waiting for him. Waiting, waiting, waiting. He'd done so much of that in the Army. He'd thought that once the war ended he would no longer have the feeling that the present was to be endured. The future was when life would really start. But it didn't feel that way for a New England boy living mostly in a hotel in Tallahassee, Florida.

Things were not going well for Jackie. She

was upset, and he didn't blame her.

Darn that guy Darryl Norwood. Ted was furious, not so much about the possible destruction of the river but the fact that some lowlife redneck was exploiting his wife by calling the new development Dreamsville Estates. That was nerve, even by Yankee standards. So much for Southern honor! Ted had a strong desire to settle the dispute the way it was done in the Army — by presenting Darryl Norwood with a knuckle sandwich right to the jawbone.

On Jackie's behalf, Ted had swallowed his pride and talked to his boss Mr. Toomb. Unfortunately, but not surprisingly, the old geezer refused to interfere with Darryl Norwood, shrewdly pointing out that if Darryl's development was successful, the airline would be, too.

Mr. Toomb, however, agreed that Ted could use his connections and time on the job to try to find out more about Darryl's backers. So Ted figured that on his monthly trip up north, he would make the short drive from New York to this place called Basking Ridge, New Jersey, and see if he could get some background and, ideally, maybe even meet the investors — information that Jackie wanted as well.

Ted wondered what it was about Jackie

that made her get in over her head. He wanted to help her, and he wanted to be on her team, but he'd come to realize that part of being married to her was coping with her impulsive side. Had she been like this in Boston? He couldn't even remember anymore. The past two years in Collier County overshadowed all the years that came before.

Meanwhile, the kids were getting older. His daughters were in a perpetual state of warfare with Jackie, and although this was worrisome Jackie assured him it was normal for teenage girls. Judd spent much of his time steering clear of his sisters and Jackie when he could, but the result was that the boy was basically raising himself. He'd joined Civil Air Patrol, and he'd been looking after Dora Witherspoon's turtles, so he was busy. But he needed a father's guidance. A father who was home.

Ted had hoped his family would adjust, and until this new problem with Darryl Norwood there'd been some progress. When they arrived in the summer of '62, he and Jackie had the worst fight they'd ever had. If only she hadn't encountered that palmetto bug sitting on the toilet seat on the very first night in their new home. After the screaming was over she'd said, "Ted, we need to talk about this *palace* you've brought us to *here* in this *cultural mecca.*"

Judd had settled in fairly quickly. But for Jackie and his daughters, it was a struggle. At least, Ted reasoned, the girls had each other. After all, they were twins. But they were not happy; anyone could see that. As for Jackie, she'd had some spectacularly bad moments but at least she'd made some friends with that book club. And ever since she'd put Naples on the map with her *Miss Dreamsville* radio show — which, thank God she wasn't doing anymore — the local people seemed more tolerant. For a while, she'd even been something of a hero.

The fact that Ted was old Mr. Toomb's right-hand man had given the family a little extra leeway. No one in town wanted to provoke Mr. Toomb, one of the richest and most powerful men south of the Mason-Dixon line, with money invested in cotton, orange groves, tobacco, sugarcane, and — that old Southern favorite — land. Mr. Toomb would stray from Ted's carefully constructed business plan and buy a piece of land, and Ted would ask why. There was never a reason beyond, "Well, it was for sale." The last time it happened, though, Mr. Toomb put Ted in his place by saying, "I hired you to give me the know-how into the way business works in the North, not to tell me what to do."

So Ted had learned to walk a thin line. He was still trying to figure out what worked and what didn't. Up north, the best way to stay gainfully employed was to play the game. Generally speaking, this meant giving your boss all the credit publicly and then you'd be rewarded later. Ted had tried that with Mr. Toomb, and it hadn't worked. He was baffled until he began to notice that in the South an employee seemed to fall into one of two categories: You were either a servant with no rights or say whatsoever or you were "family." You didn't have to be related. In fact, you could be any color of the rainbow and possibly be referred to as "family" by a white person (although never, Ted observed, the other way around). To Ted's Northern ears, there was something patronizing about a white person referring to a black person (usually a longtime servant) as "part of the family."

Then the day came when Mr. Toomb said to him, "Ted, you're like a son to me. You're a part of the family." And Ted felt very special and very honored, until he remembered that Mr. Toomb said the same thing to his longtime, long-suffering chauffeur, who was black.

He had discussed it that night with Jackie,

who was just as confused and disturbed as he was. She relayed a conversation she'd overheard two women having at the Book Nook. In loud voices they'd said, "You know, Yankees have their race problem, too. They shouldn't be coming down south telling us what to do about our Negroes." Jackie was pretty sure she was meant to overhear this remark, and was about to say something when Judd and the twins entered the store. She had planned to meet them there and buy each one a book of their choosing.

"So you didn't say anything?" Ted was surprised.

Jackie had sighed. "I'm learning to choose my battles," she'd said, "and I didn't want to embarrass the twins. But I talked to all three kids about it later at home. I asked them to think about it and I'm proud to say that all three of them had the same reaction. The phrase 'our Negroes' made them nuts."

Our Negroes. Yes, Ted had heard it many times, too. Another common saying which jarred his Yankee sensibility was "Here in the South, Negroes know their place." And the people saying it didn't seem to realize how they sounded. What was brazen and insulting to his ears was normal chitchat to them.

It was a huge relief to him that Jackie was being more careful about what she said and did. Three civil rights workers — two of them white — had been murdered three months ago in Mississippi. Even with Jackie being more prudent, he wished he was at home more, not that he could control Jackie but at least to keep a close eye on her.

Jackie complained often that she hated how much he was on the road. If she was in a particularly bad mood, he would get the "it's not easy being a woman" rant. Clearly, she was restless being a housewife and mother. Well, it wasn't so great being a man, either. That's what he wanted to say but didn't because starting a third world war was not in anyone's best interests. But was it really so bad for women? It was men who were sent off to war. It was men who died in battle or came home and had to live with what they'd seen or done. And then what? A man had to get training or an education, find a job, earn money to support a family. Sometimes he actually envied Jackie. When the kids were at school she had time on her hands. When was the last time he had that luxury? She loved that book, *The Feminine Mystique,* but he blamed it for leading to her breakdown in early '63. He would never forget how she took off in the family station wagon only to return hours later in that 1960 Buick LeSabre convertible. He understood that it was her personal declaration of independence, a way of defying the "drudgery" (her word) of her boring life as a wife and mother. What about him? What if he traded in his dull sedan for a sports car? That would be the day! Frankly he didn't feel so fulfilled, either. She wasn't the one who had to put on a suit every day and duke it out in the white-collar trenches.

Ted was surprised that the world of business felt so similar to the Army. Mr. Toomb could be as insufferable as any general, and Ted was a lowly foot soldier being sent to do the hard part, or so it seemed. And who knew the airline industry would be so awful? People thought it was glamorous, but it was like running a bus company, except these buses had wings and flew in the sky and, therefore, presented a lot more risk. The pilots were proud and stubborn, and completely unwilling to have their authority challenged. They had survived the war. Surely they didn't need "babysitting," as they called it.

But the pilots proved to be a little too casual for Ted's (and the guv-mint's) taste. They didn't worry about running low on fuel. Crash-landing? Oh, not to worry. Did that all the time during the war.

Worst of all was the shell-shocked former bomber pilot who forgot to put down the landing gear and slid to a stop — with a plane full of passengers — near the airport terminal (as these buildings were unfortunately called, in Ted's opinion) at Jacksonville. The pilot's only comment was, "Oops. Crappy landing."

Ted was beginning to think the airline wouldn't make it to the end of the year. It was now early September 1964. The incorporation papers hadn't even been signed — a "detail" (Mr. Toomb's word) that made Ted sick with anxiety. They shouldn't even have been flying. And yet Mr. Toomb was concocting ridiculous plans for expansion. To himself, Ted wondered if it was time to get his résumé ready, just in case.

SEVENTEEN

I didn't have my phone turned back on in my cottage because I thought I'd be turning right around and heading back to Mississippi. At least, that's what I told Jackie and the rest, but the truth was a little more complicated. First, I couldn't really afford it. Second, I didn't necessarily want to be reached. It seemed to me that if people really wanted to see me, they would come and sit on my porch. People who called generally just complicated my life. They wanted something. As Mama used to say, "Sometimes a phone is more trouble than it's worth."

Still, I'd encounter folks at the Winn-Dixie. My old Sunday School teacher, Mrs. Stanley, always seemed to be in the baking aisle when I made my erratic excursions for the few necessities I needed. Maybe she just camped out there, every day for hours, so she could start a conversation with someone. Of course, being a dutiful member of Olde Cypress Methodist Church, Mrs. Stanley was a prolific baker. All Methodists love to bake. Mama used to say there wasn't a Methodist alive that didn't have a big ol' sweet tooth. At Olde Cypress, it was said there was never a meeting — and they loved meetings — without some homemade goody and a pot of coffee. Maybe Mrs. Stanley truly did need to be there in the baking aisle eleven times a week, responding to an emergency request from the preacher's wife for a pineapple upside-down cake or some Collier County cheese grits. And she would have done it, too, because Mrs. Stanley was one of those church ladies who responds when duty calls.

So there she was, moseying around the flour and sugar aisle. I made a quick dash behind a display of canned green beans but, alas, Mrs. Stanley was faster than a Chihuahua that smells a chicken bone. Mama would have been ashamed of me for trying to duck from Mrs. Stanley, but my life was messy and small talk was not my forte.

"Oh, Miss Dora!" she shrieked. "I put a note in your mailbox not more than an hour ago. We just got a new shipment of Advent calendars for the children and I need someone to open the boxes and get them ready.

And it's time to plan Christmas dinner for the needy."

Advent calendars? Christmas dinner? It was mid-September. I'd been home for three weeks. To me, Christmas was far off in the distance, somewhere on the horizon. I didn't even want to think about Christmas. But to Mrs. Stanley, bless her heart, this meant she was running far behind. She was the type who started getting Easter linens out of mothballs before some folks had even taken down their Christmas lights. I spluttered, trying to buy time, but failed to come up with an excuse. I had helped her with many little tasks over the years and it seemed that in Naples, if you'd ever agreed to do something charitable, it was pretty much guaranteed that you'd be doing it for the rest of your life. You'd be in the boneyard before they let you off the hook.

These thoughts were so unkind that I felt instant remorse. I hoped Mama was busy doing something else in heaven — maybe having tea with our former neighbor, Miss Pettigrew — and not listening in on my thoughts and deeds or, sure enough, wouldn't she be ashamed of me? That was the problem with having a guardian angel sitting on your shoulder. Yes, you were protected much of the time. But it did put a certain kind of pressure on the way you behaved. To make amends to the Spirit World, I smiled at Mrs. Stanley and asked her what time I should show up.

And that is why I ended up the next day at my old Sunday School classroom, perched, with my knees halfway up to my chin, on a chair meant for a five-year-old, making lists and calculating the amount of food the church would need for Christmas donations. When I was done with that, I opened boxes filled with Advent calendars, removing them one by one from the elaborate wrapping and organizing them — as Mrs. Stanley liked — in batches of five. Mindless, yes, and yet freeing. Focusing on the simple tasks at hand, I was able to take a break from thinking about Darryl, the possibility of Dreamsville Estates, the money I would owe my landlady in Mississippi, and the important news I had discovered while I was in Jackson. News that I hadn't completely digested yet.

Going to Mississippi, all by my lonesome, had given me a new way of looking at Naples and all the folks I'd spent my life around. Sure, I'd lived in St. Petersburg when I went to junior college, and when I married Darryl we lived in Ocala. But that was all Florida. There was something about crossing the state line for the first time that made me feel like I was truly in charge of my own life. I could now say that I'd been in three states — Florida, Alabama, and Mississippi.

Now that I was home for a spell I realized that it's one thing to be stuck in your hometown and quite another to come back for a visit. It doesn't seem half as bad once you've been away. In fact, the familiarity of it — which had been suffocating — was now kind of pleasant. I mentioned this to Mrs. Stanley as we worked, side by side. She had smiled gently and said, "Sometimes you have to go away to understand the importance of what you've left behind."

After finishing my work for Mrs. Stanley, I started to head home but decided to wait an hour to hear a talk hosted by a formidable group calling itself Methodist Ladies in Action. The title was "Change Is Coming to Naples, Too!" There it was, on the bulletin board, in great big block letters.

Well, this was interesting. Living in Jackson for the past year, I was near the frontlines of the civil rights movement but I'd had the feeling since coming home that time was still passing by Naples. If there'd been protests here, they'd been small ones. The drugstore counter was still "whites only" and schools were segregated by race.

I didn't have any plans. Jackie was doing something with her kids. I had no easy way to go to Mrs. Bailey White's house and spend time with her or Plain Jane and the baby. I figured, *why not?*

The speaker was a petite lady wearing a gray suit and sensible shoes. Her hair was cropped short. No pretty bouffant and no makeup, and a smile that showed perfect teeth, a rarity in Collier County. She was introduced as a member of a church in a suburb of Cleveland with a quaint name, Shaker Heights.

She didn't waste any time getting to the point. "Let me be blunt," she said. "Your black population is not much better off than they were during the days of slavery more than a hundred years ago, and there's not much momentum here. When it comes to race relations, you're at least ten years behind Mississippi, Alabama, and Georgia."

I glanced around the room, expecting an exodus, but there was none. "You also have a migrant-worker problem inland in Immokalee," our speaker added. "Some of your seasonal farm workers are white, but many are black. And the life they are living — that includes children — is worse than anyone should be living in this country."

This was not news, especially since "Harvest of Shame," the Edwin R. Murrow special report, was broadcast by CBS the day after Thanksgiving 1960. That was nearly four years ago, and from what I'd read, the broadcast had a big impact nationally. It was a wake-up call to many Americans. Unfortunately, it was dismissed in Collier County as Northern liberal propaganda. In fact, I'd never heard anyone say anything positive about the broadcast here. What had changed in the past year was that inequality was no longer a taboo subject — at least in some circles.

The women in the audience were nodding thoughtfully. Something was happening here. I could feel it, sitting right there in the fellowship hall of the church I attended while growing up. I knew several of the women. One had been on a committee with Mama that collected funds for back-to-school clothing for poor children. With the rest, I had what was called a "nodding" acquaintance.

It was hard to know which event had broken the camel's back and galvanized these women to become something more than spectators, but if I had to guess, I'd say it was the church bombing the previous year in Birmingham, Alabama, in which four little black girls were killed. The idea that a bunch of grown men would murder children *inside a church building on a Sunday morning* would be intolerable to these women, no doubt about it.

Naples still had plenty of mean folks, including an active Klan. They were still lurking, much like Seminole Joe. The Klansmen were out there in the swamps, fields, and tidal rivers. Mama had no patience whatsoever for the Klan. As a nurse, she believed all people were the same and should be treated as such. When I was in high school, I had a long conversation with Mama about the way the world worked. "The Klan members think they're settling some kind of score from long ago," she had said. "That's just malarkey. They're just a bunch of bullies picking on colored folks for one reason: They can! They can murder colored folks, burn their churches, do what they please and no one has stopped them. That's just wrong," she said. "You remember that, Dora. It's just plain wrong. If anything, those other folks — the coloreds and the Injuns — they're the ones who ought to be settling scores, 'cause so much been done to *them* over the years. The Klan — they got it all backward."

My eyes started to tear up, as always happened when I thought about Mama. She was so wise, and I missed her so much.

"Collier County is right in the crosshairs of some of the greatest stressors in our country," the lady from Ohio was saying. That jerked me to attention. "Besides the racial problem, and the farm-worker issue, you have a new group of immigrants, the Cubans. You don't have a lot of them, mostly spillover from Miami, but they tend to find the transition to American life very difficult, especially those who were well-off in their home country and are overeducated for the jobs they can get here."

Cubans? I hadn't been aware. No one I knew had mentioned it.

"You are also perfectly positioned for explosive growth," the speaker went on. "With the growing availability of air-conditioning, you will see a large influx of people from the North."

Good Lord, I thought. *Now I'm really awake.*

"You have beautiful beaches, great fishing," she continued. "Your challenge will be managing your growth in a way that doesn't ruin what you have. And doesn't leave anyone behind."

Ha! I thought. *Ain't that the truth.*

I looked around the room again. Wouldn't

183

it have been great if the mayor had been here? Or someone from the newspaper? I wish I'd thought to call Jackie.

"I'd like to finish by saying that I wish it weren't just women in this room," our speaker said, as if reading my mind. "For some reason, men won't come to hear a woman giving a talk," she added with a slight smile.

"Well, they don't come to nothin' that's been organized by Methodist *women*," one of the organizers said, trying to sound playful. I recognized her as the wife of one of the deputy sheriffs. "I wish they would, 'cause we talk about a lot of important topics here. When we have a special guest, we always let them know they are welcome!"

I thought to myself, *That will be the day.* This led to another thought. *And we may fix all the other problems mentioned here tonight before anyone faces the fact that women aren't taken seriously.*

"Well, we can all go home and tell our men what we learned tonight," our organizer added. "If they won't come, we can always bring it to them."

What if you don't have a man? I thought. I raised my hand. The speaker nodded, and I asked my question. "Hello," I heard myself saying. "I am divorced. If you're saying we need to go home and serve our man some newfangled ideas with his breakfast grits and eggs, how do I fit in? I mean, I am just wondering. What else can women do?"

I don't know what got into me. I'd never called attention to the fact I was divorced, and now I was pointing it out in a very public way. In a room full of Methodist women, no less. I was horrified. Did I sound bitter? Sassy? Maybe even *sarcastic*? What was happening to me?

Lawd have mercy, I might have learned it from Jackie! Wasn't this a Yankee thing — not to speak up, necessarily, but to speak up *in a way that made others uncomfortable*? I surely hadn't learned this in Mississippi.

I realized all of the women in the room were staring at me. "I'm sorry," I said. "I was trying to be funny, I guess."

"Well, actually you raise a valid point," the speaker said soothingly. I was so grateful that she came to my aid that I nearly cried. "What women can do — married or not — is to speak up. Speak up at home, in church, in your civic groups, anywhere you have a chance. We are more powerful than we know, if only we make our feelings and wishes known."

Later, having retreated to my home and my turtles and their blessed unconditional love, I realized that I was, in fact, following the speaker's advice already. The unvarnished truth was that little Dora Witherspoon had changed. I was less worried about what others thought of me and more willing to speak my mind. Jackie may have had some influence, but so had the other members of the book club. Mama's death — and, no doubt, my divorce — played a role, too. I was not the same person I had been. Plus, having gone to Mississippi on my own, and having faced some truths there, gave me a certain cockiness. Heck, I was born in a small town, and I loved it, but it didn't define me. Not entirely. Not anymore.

Jackie kept writing her column, and everyone in town kept reading it. "Chatter Box" was supposed to run twice a week but Jackie, true to her nature, found it hard to be so predictable. And she didn't want to write only about Darryl. "I don't want it to seem like a vendetta," she said, so her second column was called "Mourning President Kennedy." This was a tearjerker; even those who disliked Kennedy — and there were many in Naples — had to agree that she'd really captured our nation's lingering sadness. Then she wrote one called "Why

American Schoolchildren Should Learn Foreign Languages," which got no reaction whatsoever. After that, she wrote about her beloved Buick convertible and what it meant to her, which reestablished her as a bit of a loony. (Men could wax eloquent about a cherished automobile, but it was weird for a woman to do so. The fact that it was a Buick and not a Ford or Chevy made it even more peculiar.) She told us that she wanted to write about racial hatred in the South but that her editors had asked her to wait until she was "a more seasoned columnist," which, in my estimation, was their way of saying "When hell freezes over." Finally, she got back to Darryl Norwood and Seminole Joe with a column she called "Is Dreamsville a Nightmare?"

I'd been home for almost six weeks, and while Jackie was doing some damage to Darryl, and maybe slowing him down, the sad truth was that she hadn't stopped him. Unless something totally unexpected happened, I was beginning to think that nothing could.

EIGHTEEN

Just when you think you have enough grit in your oysters, the devil has a way of upping the ante, allowing things to happen to distract or confound us mortals. Mama used to call these incidents "diversions meant to knock you off your path of righteousness." Mama surely did have a way with words, tending toward the Biblical, of course.

First, there was a little incident involving Judd Hart. He'd been one of those kids who was infatuated with the Space Race and inspired by the astronauts who were, after all, just across the state at Cape Kennedy.

Jackie got an inkling that something was amiss courtesy of the town librarian, a middle-aged woman from Sarasota with a polished appearance who had been hired to replace Miss Lansbury, who had been so helpful with Jackie's book club. One day, the new librarian called Jackie out of the blue. "I thought you should know that your son has checked out a book on explosives," she said in a crisp, yet not accusing voice. Jackie, squelching an urge to tell her that it was no one's business what anyone checked out of a library, thanked her for the information. Jackie fretted and fumed, and when Judd walked in a half hour later, she met him at the door demanding an explanation. Judd assured her that he was working on a science experiment for school and that he was trying for an A.

Later, she said she should have known better because Judd had said, "They're just *small* rockets, not like the ones on TV." And then the time-honored red flag, *"Don't worry, Mom."*

The first calls to the sheriff came from Mr. Cuthbert "Birdie" Gertleson who thought Communists from Cuba were making a land assault on Collier County. Birdie was — thank you, Jesus — unharmed but his frantic phone call and the words "missile attack!" sent the police into combat mode. Within minutes every able-bodied man in Naples was unlocking his gun cabinet, loading a shotgun, and heading for old Birdie's modest homestead.

Instead of Commies, however, all they found was Judd Hart looking guilty as a Sunday School teacher sipping moonshine.

Two other boys were hightailing it into the swamp.

Everything had gone perfectly, Judd explained, until the rocket tipped over at the last second. Instead of going up into the sky in a blaze of glory it raced horizontally across a grassy piece of tidal marsh. Incredibly, it managed to hit the only house within a half mile in any direction, the simple structure owned by Birdie Gertleson. Worse, when it hit the outside wall, it kept going. And going. Not until after it was all over did the police learn that Judd's rocket, which featured a solid brass nose cone, had careered around Birdie's living room, ripping the newspaper he was reading right out of his hands while he sat in his favorite chair, terrorizing his cat, and finally bursting through the roof.

The fact that Old Birdie wasn't dead surprised everyone, himself especially. He was so glad he wasn't dead, and that it wasn't Commies that had been attacking his humble abode, that he forgot to be angry. The cat, which is all that Birdie cared about anyway, was retrieved from its hiding place underneath Birdie's rusted 1929 Ford. Birdie's relief did not appease the sheriff, however. Judd was two inches away from being arrested.

Ted Hart had been enjoying a rare day working close to home when a Florida Highway Patrol officer, wearing the familiar Confederate pink uniform, marched into Collier County Savings & Loan where Ted and his boss Mr. Toomb were meeting with the trustees. Without time even to call Jackie, Ted was escorted to "the scene of the crime," as the officer called it, without elaboration other than somehow it involved Judd.

The sheriff was already there. Once Ted realized that no one, including Judd, had been injured, he felt a wave of relief he'd experienced only one other time in his life — when Japan surrendered and the war was finally over. He'd gotten drunk with his friends and whooped and hollered until they all passed out, exhausted.

This time, however, although he wanted to shout with joy, he hid his true feelings. He was scared of what the law would do to Judd.

So Ted did what a father was expected to do: He turned and yelled at his son. He made Judd apologize to Birdie and promise he would pay for repairs. And then he threatened to send Judd to military school, a place called Admiral Farragut Academy in St. Petersburg, which was widely believed by Judd and other boys his age to be a reform school for kids from families with financial resources.

Satisfied that Judd had been properly shamed, the trooper and the sheriff decided to let the matter rest. Justice would be served at home by the boy's father. The sheriff asked the dispatcher to send Harry Donahue from Harry's Handyman Service to secure the house and make an estimate for repairs for Ted; then he took Old Birdie and his cat to the Naples Beach Club Hotel, where they would stay, at Ted's expense, until the house was livable again. Meanwhile, the trooper agreed to drop Ted and Judd off at home.

"You are going to be mowing lawns for the rest of your life," Ted told Judd on the way home, "and every penny will pay me back for all these expenses."

"Do I really have to go to military school?" Judd asked, wide-eyed.

Aware that the trooper was listening, Ted said yes. But he knew that Jackie would never let that happen. Judd figured the same. Considering that he could have found himself in juvenile jail, Judd was rather pleased overall with the outcome of the day's events. Mowing lawns would be no problem. In fact, he already had a lawn-mowing service with more than a dozen regular customers. So what if he was essentially working for his dad for a while? He'd gotten off easy.

The second unnerving event came in the form of a letter hand-delivered to Mrs. Bailey White's. Jackie had just finished telling us about Judd's "misadventure," as she phrased it. She had missed all the excitement involving the rocket fiasco, having driven the twins to voice lessons with a Mrs. Pendergast in Punta Gorda. "Here I was trying to be a good mother to my girls, and when we come home I find out my son has turned into a mad scientist!" she groaned, blotting her eyes with a tissue. "I had my children when I was too young! I am a complete catastrophe as a mother!"

"Oh, now, stop being a Miss Melodrama," Mrs. Bailey White said. "Have a Dr Pepper and calm down."

"Ugh," Jackie said with disgust. "I hate that Dr Pepper stuff. Do you have any tonic water? Better yet, some gin to go with it?"

"Too early in the day," Plain Jane scolded. "With this heat you'll end up with a huge headache."

"Ted went to New Orleans and he said all the people there drink even in the late morning," Jackie said defensively.

"Honey child, this ain't no *New Orleans,*" Mrs. Bailey White said, shaking her head. "That's up north compared to here. We're in the *tropics.* Besides, those folks are party-goers. They got pickle juice in their veins. But they don't live as long as we do. By the way, did you know they don't bury their people in the ground?"

"Well, what do they do with them?" Jackie asked.

"They bury 'em *above* ground. They call them 'mausoleums.'"

"Oh, yes," Jackie said. "I've seen photographs of that. I think it's because the water table there is so high."

A knock at the door made us jump nearly out of our skins. In a way I was grateful because the conversation was giving me the creepy-crawlies.

"I'll get it," I said, but by the time I reached the door I wished I'd let someone else answer it. Through the scalloped lace curtain on the windowpane beside the front door, I could see a silhouette of the distinctive hat worn by a police officer in uniform. I cracked open the door, and he thrust a letter into my hand without saying a word.

"Wait," he said, as I started to close the door. "Someone has to sign for it." This made me even more uneasy, but I did as I was told.

"Dora?" Mrs. Bailey White called out. "Who is it, dear?"

I returned to the parlor. "Oh, it's nothing, probably. Just a letter from the town."

"Mrs. Bailey White, did you pay your taxes?" Plain Jane said, alarmed.

"Course I did! Don't know what this nonsense could be. Dora, dear, you open it and read it aloud, okay?"

I was beginning to think that Jackie's gin and tonic suggestion might be a good one. "All right," I said, my voice squeaky. "Well, let's see. It's addressed to you and date-stamped today — October 10, 1964. It says":

Dear Matilda Louise Bailey White:
It has come to our attention that you have exceeded the number of unrelated persons living in this house, and that one of the residents is a child unrelated to any of the residents. You are, therefore, running a rooming house and/or child care institution without proper permit.

"What else does it say?" Jackie asked, after she recovered enough to speak. "Is there a court date? Do we pay a fine?"

"It's a warning," Plain Jane said.

"Can we ignore it?" Jackie asked. "In Boston if you get a letter like that, you just ignore it. Nine times out of ten, that's the end of it."

"I don't think we can do that," Plain Jane said. "I think we'll have to address it in some way." She thought for a moment and added, "Well, I suppose it's not surprising. They always find a way to get to you."

"Who?" Jackie asked. "You mean Darryl?"

"Yes, Darryl. And maybe his backers, too. Those people from that place in New Jersey."

Mrs. Bailey White nodded. "He's fighting dirty," she said.

"We don't know that for sure," I said, but the second the words left my lips I realized it was probably true. Plain Jane, Jackie, and Mrs. Bailey White had been looking after Dream for more than a year. There had been complaints but nothing had really come of it. This felt like retribution.

We discussed what we should do. As Mama would have said, we talked that ol' topic to death and right into the next world. Finally, we agreed to face it head-on by going to the municipal offices. The plan was that we'd go together. By now it was late in the day so we decided to meet at 8:30 sharp the next morning outside the town-owned trailer, adjacent to the police station.

The first accusation in the letter to Mrs. Bailey White turned out to be easy to disprove. Jackie, Plain Jane, and I were able to demonstrate that we were only "visitors" at the house owned by Mrs. Bailey White. For Jackie, it was as easy as handing them her driver's license with her home address on it. Plain Jane and I, who didn't drive, brought our property tax bills with us.

"But what about the girl?" The clerk, a plump gal with a beehive hairdo, posed the question as if she was sure we were hiding something.

"What girl?" Plain Jane asked.

"The colored girl," the clerk said, snapping gum in her mouth. "The one who comes to stay there. And her colored baby."

Clearly, the clerk had been apprised of every detail. "What, are you guys spying on us?" Jackie said, in her usual "anything but subtle" way.

"No one's spying on anyone," the clerk snapped. "But we have become aware that a colored girl about age twenty stays in that house from time to time. And her baby is there *all* the time. Is it their legal residence?"

The question caught us off-guard. "The girl's legal address is at her grandmother's,"

Mrs. Bailey White said. "And the baby's, too." Whether or not this was true, I didn't know, but it was a good answer.

The clerk sighed. "All right," she said. "Looks like you've satisfied the first part of the complaint. But not the second. If that baby isn't related to any of you, and you have no legal status in her life, then she shouldn't be living there. Unless you have a license for some kind of school or maybe a home for unwed mothers and their babies, something like that."

A smile that I recognized as mischievous suddenly appeared on Jackie's face. "Well, thank you *so very much*!" Jackie gushed to the clerk. "You've been *so very helpful*!"

Jackie practically skipped out the door.

"What are you so happy about?" Plain Jane asked warily.

"That gal in there just handed us the solution!" she said. "All we have to do is open a house for unwed mothers and babies. It's that simple! We can keep Dream and maybe help some other young women, too."

"Whoa, wait a minute," Plain Jane said.

"What do you think, Mrs. Bailey White?" Jackie asked, adding, "Of course, this is entirely up to you."

Mrs. Bailey White looked overwhelmed but smiled. "I don't know how much good

I'll be to y'all," she said slowly, "but you're welcome to use my house."

"I admit that it's a fascinating idea," Plain Jane said cautiously, "but Jackie, aren't you getting ahead of yourself? You always have us rushing into things!"

"Dora, what do you think?" Jackie asked, ignoring Plain Jane.

"Well, I won't be here. I still plan to go back to Mississippi," I said. "But if y'all think you can do it, I don't see why not. Of course, there's something you're forgetting. We need to talk to Priscilla first. She should be told what's going on. She would need to be on board with this."

It was agreed. Jackie would try to reach Priscilla by telephone and report back to us the next day.

As I nodded off to sleep that night, I marveled at Jackie's enthusiasm and her ability to find answers while I was still busy mulling over the question. She was persuasive, and made things sound easier than they were — like talking me into going to Mississippi to find out about Mama and her people. Once you've known someone like Jackie, however, you can't easily go back to a life in which you're sitting on the sidelines, waiting for something to happen. Before I knew her, I thought the best way to travel through life was to take the most comforting and familiar routes. While I still longed to do this at times — it was part of my nature — I could see now that playing it too safe might mean never really living at all. From Jackie, I had learned to take the plunge into the deep end of the pond, not just stick my toe in, or wade around in the shallows.

NINETEEN

As the Trailways bus rambled toward Naples, Priscilla yawned politely and stretched, taking care not to bump into the older woman sitting next to her. She reminded Priscilla a little of her grandma — tiny and hunched over, with hands swollen and disfigured from a lifetime of working in the fields.

Priscilla had been trying to read on the long bus ride from Daytona, with some success on the Sanford to Tampa stretch, but then began dozing off, tired from working late in the college laundry. One employee went home sick, so she'd been doing the job of two people but complaining was unthinkable. Working until midnight — even in a hot and humid laundry — was easy compared to what her grandma did, day after day.

The older woman suddenly elbowed her and cried out, pointing to something outside the bus window. Even wedged as they were in the far-back seat of the colored section, it was hard to miss: a brand-new, oversized billboard with lime-green lettering.

Welcome to Dreamsville! the sign hollered.

What in the world? Priscilla thought.

And then they passed another, identical to the first. This time, Priscilla got more than a glimpse. Accompanying the astonishing words was a stylized illustration of an idealized American couple. A white gal was tastefully reclined in a lounge chair with a long cigarette in one hand and a cute little mixed drink — the kind with an umbrella in it — beside her on a small table. A white fellow, presumably her husband, loomed in the foreground with an expensive-looking fishing pole in one hand and a golf club in the other, grinning so broadly it was scary. *Lord,* Priscilla thought, *you'd think God himself had just handed him the keys to the Kingdom of Heaven. Imagine going through life with that amount of self-assurance.* The couple, to Priscilla's eyes, looked vaguely Northern. For one thing, they were tan. With the exception of men who worked outdoors — a farmer with his red neck from driving a tractor, or a fisherman with deep crows'-feet wrinkles acquired from squinting at the water — local white folks protected their skin from the sun. In fact, it was said among black folks that the Caucasians of Collier County were so white that looking at them hurt your eyes. Priscilla tried not to join in when others joked like that. White folks couldn't help being white any more than she could help the fact that she was not. Besides, she'd been treated exceptionally well by white folks. Most of them, anyway.

The other indication that the folks depicted in the sign were supposed to be Yankees was, in a word, jewelry. The gal on the lounge chair had a ring on one hand that would have made Elizabeth Taylor pass out, plus ropes of gold, pearls, and who-knows-what hanging heavily around her neck. All this, and wearing a bathing suit, too. The man, who wore a polo shirt with some kind of insignia like a family crest or college logo, sported an oversized watch on one wrist.

In sociology class, Priscilla had learned that these folks were called "the Northern Leisure Class." But why would they come to Naples? Who was putting out the welcome mat?

And why were there so many? Unlike the South, where there were a handful of rich folks in every small town — with everyone else poor as dirt — there seemed to be a surplus of people with money to burn in Yankeeland. She couldn't imagine being able to afford one house, let alone one up north and a second one in Florida just for vacations. Vacations! That was a concept she couldn't grasp, either. Life was not a cakewalk for anyone, her granny used to counsel, but sometimes it sure seemed that way from the outside looking in.

When the bus passed a third, identical billboard, this time Priscilla noticed the words "Coming Soon!" on a banner that stretched across the lower right corner. Well, whatever was going on, it probably wasn't good, and Priscilla felt a cool chill move down her spine like someone had just walked over an unsettled grave.

Jackie had not said a word on the telephone about any of this. Did she not know? Or did she not care? No, Jackie would care. She would be angry, unless she was involved in it in some way. But why would she be involved? Jackie wouldn't like the idea of someone using "Dreamsville" without her permission, and Priscilla couldn't imagine Jackie accepting payment for it, or endorsing a development of some sort, either. That didn't seem like Jackie's style.

Of course, maybe Jackie hadn't mentioned it because long-distance calls cost a pretty penny. More than that, though, was a lack of privacy on Priscilla's end. With more than fifteen girls sharing one phone at the rooming house that was Priscilla's home-away-from-home at Bethune-Cookman College, someone always seemed to be lurking in the hallway awaiting her turn. Opportunities were ripe for eavesdropping. The other complication was that Priscilla, working in the laundry and attending classes, often missed Jackie's calls. It was remarkable how much information a nosy floor-mate could glean from a simple phone message, so Jackie quickly learned to avoid chitchat and to leave a message saying only that Priscilla needed to call home.

Whenever Priscilla found one of these messages stuck in the doorjamb of her little room, she felt a little faint. Without fail, she was at first convinced that something had happened to her baby. Maybe Dream was sick and desperately needed her mama. A negligent, selfish, fool-hearted mama who was clear across the state, and almost as far north as the Georgia border, studying English and sociology at a black college where no one knew her secret.

The hallway was silent, thanks to the late hour, so Priscilla dropped her book bag and purse and dashed to the phone to call Jackie back. As always she asked the long-distance operator to reverse charges, which made her feel wretched until she forced herself to remember her baby daughter. She was doing this for her child. She would do anything for her child. That was why she was away, to build a better life for herself and, in turn, for Dream.

She felt the same way the next morning when she sat in the back of the Trailways bus. She was doing that for Dream, too. Nine years after Mrs. Parks refused to move from the white section of a bus in Birmingham, the colored section was business as usual in Florida. Here it was 1964, the Civil Rights Act had just been signed by President Johnson, and the yellow line that designated the "back of the bus" was as bright and menacing as ever. There were times when Priscilla could sit wherever she wanted, especially if the bus was nearly empty. But if a bus driver was a bigot, he'd tell you to go to the back of the bus. Or, if there were mean-looking white passengers — and you could never tell, really, just from a glance — it was better to go sit in the back of the bus and live to talk about it. This stuck in Priscilla's craw and she felt that familiar flash of soul-crushing shame, but again, just like those collect calls, they could be tolerated if she was doing it for her child.

Jackie had declared that Priscilla should sit wherever she wanted when she rode the bus, but Jackie was a Northerner. More to the point, Jackie was white. What did she know of such things? It was Plain Jane, the poet who paid her bills by writing for strange magazines, who made Priscilla promise to be cautious. Plain Jane, a progressive-minded Southerner although she didn't look it with her conservative clothes and steel-gray hair that matched her eyes. "Don't listen to Jackie on this," she had told Priscilla in a hushed voice on one of her visits home. "You do what you have to."

Old Mrs. Bailey White had overheard and quickly agreed. "Get yourself through college," she counseled. "That's your job right now. Keep your focus, and don't get in no fusses."

These words of advice made all the difference. It was still hard. Hard to accept their charity for those bus tickets home and for taking care of Dream. But Priscilla was what her granny called "an old soul," meaning that from the day of her birth she seemed wise beyond her years, as if she'd lived one long life already. She didn't have all the answers, and she made mistakes, but God had given her the gift of resilience. That, and a very unyouthful tendency to be a good listener when it came to advice, made her seem much older than her nineteen-and-a-half years.

This was an odd arrangement. Unheard of, as a matter of fact, and yet it seemed to be working. There'd been a rough patch a few months earlier when Priscilla learned that her friends had endured some abusive remarks when they were out and about with Dream. At that point, Priscilla was prepared to come home for good. She would live with her grandma and do her best to raise Dream.

Plain Jane and Mrs. Bailey White had straightened out the situation, however. They understood that most Southerners would look the other way unless provoked. Privacy and minding your own business trumped speaking up and interfering. The problem was Jackie, who was in the habit of driving around town with Dream in that crazy convertible. She would take Dream with her into the Winn-Dixie and when people stared she'd say, "What's the matter, haven't your ever seen a black child with a white nanny before?" And then she'd laugh out loud.

Naturally, that got folks stirred up. And it

wasn't necessary. So on one of Priscilla's trips home, the remnants of the little book club had a discussion. There was a whole lot of finger-pointing, with Plain Jane and Mrs. Bailey White taking sides against Jackie. Poor Jackie had this harebrained idea that she was somehow helping the civil rights movement. Finally, after hearing them out, Priscilla spoke her mind. It was hard to think of the right words. She prayed to God to help her find them.

"Jackie," she began slowly. Having been in the book club together, they all knew what it meant when Priscilla spoke cautiously. It meant she was trying to think of a way to say something powerful without hurting too many feelings. "Jackie," she began again, "you know I love you and that I am indebted to you for making it possible for me to go to college. And I know that your heart is in the right place when it comes to helping my people. But you are endangering my child."

There it was, like a bomb had gone off. *You are endangering my child.* Those were words harsh but true.

Of course, Jackie had reacted like someone had dumped a bucket of wet collard greens over her head. Priscilla couldn't even bear to look at her. But she had said what needed to be said.

Plain Jane, who quarreled with Jackie on a fairly regular basis, could not resist adding her two cents. "I told you so," she said to Jackie. "You were flaunting that baby around like that, just to make a point —"

"Ladies, please," Mrs. Bailey White interrupted. "Let's all calm down and remember we are friends. We are all in this together. Jackie didn't mean any harm. She just don't understand sometimes, that's all."

Jackie said nothing for the next hour, maybe longer, and avoided eye contact with all of them. Priscilla, meanwhile, had been consumed with despair, thinking she had been rude and ungrateful, and had pushed too far.

Plain Jane and Mrs. Bailey White talked about the baby, how much she had grown, about her sleep habits, and how cute she was, in far more depth than was necessary. Finally, Plain Jane addressed Jackie. "Didn't you say that Dream was the smartest little thing you ever saw?" she prompted.

Jackie cleared her throat. "Yes, I think she is very advanced. And since I'm the only one here — other than Priscilla, of course — who is a mother, I do think I know what I'm talking about."

"Of course you do," Priscilla had said quickly.

"No one is questioning your instincts or experience," Plain Jane said. "It's just that you're a foreigner here, you don't understand how to behave —"

"A foreigner! Why, excuse me, but I thought we were all citizens of the United States of America. I didn't realize I needed a *passport* to live in the Confederate State of Florida."

This was getting nasty but at least it signaled to Priscilla that Jackie was not upset or angry with her. Just the entire South.

No one, even Jackie, wanted to take this conversation any further. "Priscilla," she said bluntly, "I will reign in my boorish Yankee *behavior* but I will do it for your sake, and for Dream's. Not for any other reason. And not because I'm wrong."

Six or seven months had passed and Jackie had held to her promise. No more driving around town with Dream. The baby was transported, and taken out in public, only when necessary. And, no more comments about being a white nanny. As Plain Jane and Mrs. Bailey White predicted, the rumor mill ground to a halt. People didn't really care as long as they didn't have their noses rubbed in it. Their attention was focused elsewhere, on some other unlucky target.

But now the problem had suddenly flared up again. That was the gist of the conversation when Jackie made the latest phone call. When Priscilla got the message and called back, Jackie seemed to be waiting by the telephone. "There is a new problem with us taking care of Dream," she whispered into the phone. Specifically, she said, that the baby was "residing" at Mrs. Bailey White's house.

And so Priscilla had asked the college's dean of women students for an emergency leave. Eyebrows were raised, but Priscilla managed to convey in the vaguest of terms that there was a family emergency without providing details that would get her expelled.

As the bus pulled away from Daytona Beach, Priscilla said her silent good-bye to the little city on the Atlantic coast where people drove cars on the beach, and to the college where all the students looked like her, and no one thought it delusional to dream of becoming an English teacher or anthropologist. Each time she left, she wrestled with the feeling that perhaps she might never be back.

TWENTY

Blast those old war pilots, Ted Hart thought with disgust. He knew it was wrong to think that way about his fellow veterans, but they were still making it awfully hard to bring civilization to Florida.

He was beginning to suspect that some of them enjoyed rough landings. More than once, he'd heard them laughing and boasting about cutting things a little close.

"This is a *business* and these are *passengers*," Ted implored after another complaint.

The pilots responded in nearly identical ways. "Well, that's the way we flew in the war and we survived, so don't tell us how to fly," they'd say. "Especially since you were a foot soldier, fella. Your kind doesn't know the first thing about flying."

The latter part was true. Ted didn't even know how to fly a kite. But he was in charge and he figured these guys should listen to him. He'd have fired them all but they were the only qualified pilots who had applied. A few crop dusters had answered the ads and while they didn't make the grade, Ted secretly wondered if they might not have done a better job from a customer-service perspective.

On one particularly awful day, a pilot failed to secure the nose hatch on a plane flying south from Tampa. Unfortunately, the hatch sprang open in midflight, sending air-bags belonging to the U.S. Postal Service straight into the right engine propeller. The result was a shower of shredded mail dispersed over Fort Myers, followed by an engine fire which resulted in a noteworthy emergency landing on a golf course.

Meanwhile, Mr. Toomb was starting to lean harder on Ted. None of the routes, which now crisscrossed the state, were making a profit and were not likely to for months. Most of the airports were not up to par, and several lacked hangar space for planes bigger than a two-seater Beechcraft. Ted needed to persuade local officials that Wild Blue Yonder Airways would be a boon to their communities. He traveled the state with mixed results. At times, officials wouldn't even meet with him unless Mr. Toomb called first on his behalf. Finally,

Ted found his niche. When the mayor of Daytona Beach mentioned he was going on a fishing trip to Crescent City, the "Bass Capital," Ted remarked that he'd spent several summers on a fishing boat out of Gloucester, Massachusetts. Next thing Ted knew, he was invited not only to fish for bass by the Daytona Beach mayor but to go deep-sea fishing with the mayor of Fort Lauderdale. As word got out that Ted not only liked to fish but was quite good at it, he found doors opening to his sales pitch. His wardrobe of navy blue suits was pushed to the back of the closet.

Jackie wasn't thrilled with this development. In fact, she was furious. "Oh, Ted, where are you going this week?" she would ask on Sunday nights. "Shall we pack your new Brooks Brothers suit, or would you prefer your *fishing regalia*?"

Try as he might, he wasn't able to convince her that he was, in fact, working. "This is the way I have to do business here," he would say. But she would give him what he thought of as "the look," a sideways glance of her suddenly chilly blue eyes. What he hesitated to tell her was that he ought to be working on his golf game, too.

He tried to interest Jackie with stories from his time on the road. Sometimes she was so resentful of his being away that she didn't want to hear them. But there were other times — the best times — when he and Jackie talked late into the night about this surprising place called Florida. The biggest shock had been learning that the state was, in fact, a part of the South.

From a Bostonian's point of view, America consisted of Northern and Southern states, the Great Plains and the West Coast. Of course, there were subcategories: New England was one, but also border states (people who could not make up their mind which side of the Civil War they were on), the Deep South (a place where cotton was grown and people walked barefoot all the time), Texas (cowboys, the Alamo, oil rigs), the Rockies (extremely tall mountains), Chicago (a notable area of civilization in the vast and confusingly laid-out Midwest), California (Hollywood people), and Seattle (so far away that it was exotic). Hawaii? That was a honeymoon destination for the well-heeled. And Alaska? A place that got more snow than Boston and had an unusual variety of wild animals.

That pretty much left Florida, a place that didn't fit into any category except its own. More than thirteen hundred miles of coastline gave the impression that the whole state

216

was a tropical paradise. Many inland communities, however, were afflicted by the type of Deep South poverty Ted had thought existed only in states such as Alabama or Mississippi, or in the Appalachian Mountains of Kentucky. This inland poverty affected both whites and blacks. It was the one thing the two races had in common.

Ted felt badly for blacks living in Florida — especially those living inland. They often had a sort of downcast look, like they were trapped and knew it was hopeless. The sorrow in their eyes reminded him of the displaced persons he had seen in Europe, civilians who had lost everything in the war and had nowhere to go.

At least the black people seemed to be living in reality, Ted thought. He was not so sure about the whites. Like an episode of the TV show *The Twilight Zone,* many white people acted as if someone had set their clocks back a hundred years and they hadn't noticed. Again and again, Ted would be told that Union troops had "invaded" the South, ending a perfectly decent way of life, and that colored folks were "happier in the old days." Ted concluded that white Southerners, generally speaking, were looking backward, clinging to the past with increasing desperation at the very same time that

Northerners were fixated on the future. In April, New York City had opened the 1964 World's Fair with a hopeful theme called "Peace Through Understanding." From what Ted had read in *Time* magazine, the fair focused on marvelous inventions that would make life better. But what good was any of it, he thought, if we didn't fix the big problems first, like race and poverty?

In the last year, he noted that it seemed to have become more difficult being a Yankee, unless you were a typical beach tourist. Comments were made. Looks were exchanged. Previously, his Boston accent had been tolerated or even met with friendly curiosity; now it seemed an invitation to be harassed. There was, for example, the restaurant owner in Hardee County who sat down uninvited opposite Ted and grinned menacingly. All Ted had wanted was a lousy cup of coffee and a doughnut but instead he was treated to a disgusting lecture about "the inferiority of the Negro race" and how Yankees needed to mind their own business. Ted had not taken the bait. He was expected, he knew, to get up and walk out or throw a punch but he did neither. While the old redneck droned on and on, Ted had simply pulled out a recent copy of the *Wall Street Journal* and began to read it. He munched slowly on the doughnut and, after he finished his coffee, he left.

In his free time he visited libraries and historical societies, especially when work took him to larger cities. The territory of Florida, Ted learned, had been in Spanish hands, then English, and back to Spanish again, until Spain ceded the territory to the United States in 1821. Slavery of blacks (and also Indians) was fully entrenched long before Florida became a state in 1845. When Southern slave states began to secede from the Union, starting with South Carolina in December 1860, Florida was third in line. More than 15,000 Florida troops fought for the Confederacy.

Now, this was the part Ted really wanted to know about: What happened after the Civil War? To his surprise, he found that black Floridians endured decades of intimidation and violence by whites that rivaled — *and even surpassed* — other Southern states. Ted was appalled that in one particularly heinous act, an NAACP leader named Harry T. Moore and his wife were murdered on Christmas Day 1951 in their home in the small town of Mims in Brevard County.

One thing Ted was trying to figure out was whether he should use the term colored, Negro, Afro-American, or black. After thinking it through, he started habitually using the latter since it seemed to have been the term preferred by the Massachusetts-born Dr. W. E. B. Du Bois, a black scholar and one of the founders of the NAACP who had died the previous year.

Anger and anxiety was not about race only, Ted was discovering. Longtime Floridians both black and white were increasingly at odds with the tourist industry. How could Old Florida hang onto its proud past as part of the Confederacy and remain a place that tolerated the KKK while attracting Northern tourists? By downplaying the true identity of the state and painting a lovely portrait of endless beaches, golf, and fishing. That was the truth that Ted was beginning to understand.

Meanwhile, his children, most unfortunately, were starting to speak like the local rednecks. This was worrisome. How would they ever get ahead in life? The twins insisted that if they spoke in their native tongue — that is, a Northern dialect — they would never be accepted, never get a date, and simply die of boredom. They picked up the far-south accent almost immediately, probably, Ted thought, because they were so young. Judd, too, sounded like he belonged on that TV show *The Beverly Hill-*

billies. But Judd and the twins could turn it on and off with a natural ease, depending on who they were talking to. To Ted, it was the darndest thing. He couldn't even say "y'all" without the word sounding like a chicken bone were stuck in his throat.

On one hurtful day, all three kids announced that they felt humiliated by their parents, who sounded like the Kennedys. Those Boston accents, the kids insisted, had become grating to their ears. The kids pointed out that Jackie, when she'd had her radio show, had learned from the station manager that by speaking very slowly, and dragging out the syllables, she could hide it. She was aghast that they would ask her to try to adapt her radio technique to everyday speech. No way, she said. As for Ted, he was a hopeless case. He didn't seem to be able to drop the accent even when he tried.

Jackie ended the family quarrel with a linguistic triumph: A Boston accent, she noted, was not that dissimilar from a Charleston accent. "And, heck," she said, "Charleston is in *South Carolina,* which, by anyone's definition, is a Rebel state." ("Tell *that* to your friends next time they make fun of the way your mother talks," she added.)

These were the issues Ted hadn't foreseen

when they moved here. When he was in the Army twenty years earlier, there was some teasing about accents but mostly it was good-natured. Then again, it was wartime and they were all facing a common enemy. It didn't matter if you were the son of a factory worker from Massachusetts or the son of a wealthy landowner from Tennessee. You could be a ranch hand from Texas or a college boy from Milwaukee, but when each of you was wearing a U.S. Army uniform fighting side by side against the Axis forces, you were American, that's all.

Now, for the first time in his life, Ted was self-conscious about his Northern background. In the tight smile of a waitress or the cool, perfunctory nod of a gas station attendant, he felt a wall descend the second he spoke. Sometimes he wondered if he was reliving the exact dynamics of the Civil War era, a deeply troubling thought for a man who had lived with the assumption that he would always be welcome anywhere in the USA. He had noticed more and more people calling him "Yankee," and not in a playful way. Someone leaving a bar in Tallahassee had even called him "carpetbagger," which shocked him. He trudged back to his hotel, thinking, *They'd rather live in the past and be left behind.* But he was an interloper, a harbinger of change in the same way that a mackerel sky indicates rain. If there was one thing that Southerners found disturbing, it was change. Especially, Ted had learned, when it wasn't their idea.

Twenty-One

"You know, you and me, we got a lot in common," Dolores said in the direction of the heron's nest. "Say, are you even in there? Can't see you."

A small tuft of yellow feathers slowly rose into view.

"Oh, now I see you there," Dolores said. "Out late last night, huh? I used to be like that, too."

The small head slowly sank back out of sight.

"So what I was saying," Dolores continued, "was that we have a lot in common. For one thing, I don't believe you have the slightest idea what you're doing. You shoulda had them babies earlier in the year, not now. *Hmmm,* maybe it's a second clutch of eggs. Or maybe you're just out of kilter with everyone else.

"But I have to tell you, girl," Dolores added. "I ain't seen no man around your

rupted. "We don't need some highfalutin Yankee lawyer! What we need is a local boy."

Naples was a small town and between us we quickly came up with a list of every lawyer in town. They all had ties, however, to the most powerful folks in town. Finally, we agreed that several of us should make a day trip up to Fort Myers in search of a lawyer. Whether one could be found — indeed, whether one existed — who would meet with all of our approval, and who was willing to look into our situation, would remain to be seen. But as Mama used to say, "You've got to get out there and try. Sitting at home and doing nothing but frettin' will never get you anywhere."

I did not have a dime to contribute and felt badly for it, but between Jackie, Mrs. Bailey White, and Plain Jane, there was enough to pay for a lawyer.

They returned from Fort Myers feeling triumphant, having managed to find "a nice young man who is not connected," as Jackie explained. This made me a little uneasy. "Young" could be good; passion and energy might trump experience. "Unconnected" to Jackie and the others meant "uncontaminated," but I wondered if it might translate as powerless.

The lawyer's name was John Ed Yonce. He was very interested in the case but said he'd have to meet Dolores first. This, of course, was a problem. How would we get Dolores to go to Fort Myers? Even if Jackie offered to drive her up there, we didn't think she would go.

Somehow, Jackie had persuaded poor Mr. Yonce to come to Collier County and meet Dolores at her home. I say *poor* Mr. Yonce because that fella was in over his head. I don't think there was anything he learned in law school that could have prepared him for Dolores. Or Jackie, for that matter.

Jackie offered to transport Mr. Yonce from Fort Myers to Naples if necessary but announced that she would not drive him to Dolores's fishing shack. "It's horrible for my car," she declared. "I really don't want to drive back there again." And who could blame her?

Neither Mrs. Bailey White nor Plain Jane were in a position to help. That left me to figure out what to do. I could escort him by foot or canoe. Mr. Yonce chose the latter.

The next morning, I waited at the public boat launch as agreed. The day started badly. When I tried to pay the fee to rent the canoe with a Kennedy fifty-cent piece, the man in charge refused to accept the coin on account of the fact that he was a Kennedy hater. Now, I found this disgusting for a variety of reasons. Number one, Kennedy was dead — assassinated! — and the way I was raised, "of the dead say nothing evil." Secondly, he had been our president and therefore deserved our respect whether you agreed with him or not. Last but not least, the coin was issued by our government and was therefore as legitimate as a twenty-dollar bill or anything else.

Well, I won that battle based on the last point. He took my fifty-cent piece, but I was left with a sick feeling in my stomach and an angry headache.

I was relieved when Jackie finally pulled up. A man I presumed to be Mr. Yonce sat beside her in the front seat. Was it some kind of mistake? He didn't look much older than Judd. As he climbed out of the car, my heart sank even further when I saw that he was wearing a suit and wing-tip shoes.

Jackie took off with a wave of the hand, leaving us to our own introductions.

"My, isn't she something?!" he said. "Mrs. Hart, I mean. She told me all about her radio show, how she gave that up, and now she's writing a newspaper column."

"Oh, she's something else all right," I said with a smile. Men of all ages were always impressed with Jackie. What I didn't say was, *Oh boy, if you think Jackie is something else, just wait until you meet Miss Bunny Ann McIntyre, aka Dolores Simpson.*

"Thank you for taking me today," he said.

"Mr. Yonce, um, why are you wearing . . . *those clothes?*" I asked.

"Because I'm meeting a client!" he said as if it was the most obvious thing in the world.

He put on a lifesaving vest — few of us locals wore them, even though they were made available at the dock — and climbed daintily in the canoe. I could see I had a long day ahead of me.

"Aren't you going to help me paddle?" I asked.

"I don't know how," he said.

"I'll show you how," I replied. "Get in the front."

Despite my instructions, Mr. Yonce was not much help, especially after a ten-foot gator splashed into the water from a riverbank not ten feet from us. Mr. Yonce proceeded to do exactly the wrong thing: He panicked and stood up.

"Sit down, Mr. Yonce! You'll flip us over!" I yelled.

He did as he was told, but after that he didn't try to paddle at all. After a few minutes he asked my permission to turn around and face me. I don't think he even wanted to look at the water the rest of the trip.

"Where the heck did you grow up?" I asked.

"Atlanta," he said. "Downtown. Near Peachtree Street."

Well, that explained a few things. "Whatcha doing in Florida?"

"Wanted to start somewhere new," he said. "But I didn't know it was going to be like this," he added hastily.

I started to feel sorry for him. This was always my downfall. I could not stay mad at someone I felt sorry for.

"See those trees there?" I asked, trying to distract him. "Those are called mangroves. They are incredibly adaptive —"

"What is that over there?" he asked nervously. "That thing near the mangroves."

I saw the back of a manatee bobbing in the water. "Oh, that's just a sea cow," I said reassuringly. "Don't worry, they don't eat people. They only eat vegetation. They are the gentlest creatures on earth."

"Oh," he said with a weak smile. "Glad to hear it."

With me paddling alone it took a good forty-five minutes to arrive at Dolores's dock, and, as luck would have it, she wasn't there. I tossed a rope around one of the posts and secured the canoe, not that it was going anywhere. The tide and the current were gently pushing us against the dock for now. At least something was going in our favor.

"Do we have to get out?" my passenger asked somberly.

"What? Out of the canoe? Why, yes, of course we do."

"I'd rather not," he said, looking around.

"Who's there?" Dolores bellowed from the vicinity of the outhouse. "What do y'all want?"

"Dolores," I called out, "it's me, Dora Witherspoon, and I've brought a . . . friend. He wants to meet you."

"Well, I don't want to meet *him,*" she shouted. But she was walking toward us, craning her neck to get a look at him. Another moment and she was on the dock, looming over us. Then she burst out laughing. "What's he wearing? A suit and tie? Have you lost your mind, Mr. — ?"

"—Yonce," he said automatically. "Pleased to meet you." He was still sitting in the canoe, gripping the sides.

"Mr. Yonce is an attorney," I said. "A lawyer. He's here to help us."

"I know what an attorney is," Dolores

said. "You must think I'm dumb as this post here," she said, shoving a calloused hand against one of the wood pilings, which shook slightly. The whole structure, shack and all, could come crashing down into the water for all I knew. And yet it had survived many storms, even Hurricane Donna, so perhaps the underpinnings were sturdier than they appeared.

"I do not think you're dumb and you know it," I said, a little surprised at myself for sounding so fresh. "Mr. Yonce came quite a distance to talk to you. So please hear what he has to say."

"Are y'all going to get out of this here canoe?" Dolores asked, putting her hands on her hips.

"I'm quite comfortable here," Mr. Yonce said, "but thank you so much."

Dolores stifled a chuckle. "You mean you don't want to come inside and maybe sit in my, er, *parlor?*" She laughed heartily at her own joke, which startled Peggy Sue, the night heron, who made an unhappy squawk.

"Uh-oh," I said, "now we've upset Peggy Sue."

"Peggy Sue is a bird," Dolores said to Mr. Yonce by way of explanation. "Over yon, up in a tree. She be sitting on her eggs like a good mama."

Mr. Yonce looked from Dolores to me and back again. "Yes, um, okay," he said, clearing his throat. He began talking very fast, explaining that if Dolores agreed, he could file papers that would stop Darryl from proceeding with construction until a judge could review the rightful ownership of the land.

"I have done some preliminary work," he said, "and did some research on the documents that, I understand, belong to you."

Dolores, still standing on the dock, nodded. I wondered how many lawyers had met with a client like this, sitting in a canoe and wearing a life vest.

"What I learned is that your main document is a deed put in trust, with a large amount of cash, many years ago," he said. "It's called a perpetual trust, and it was set up by General John Stuart Williams — your ancestor. The taxes have been paid automatically through the trust. Very clever idea — maybe the old general was concerned about carpetbaggers trying to grab property when the owners were late paying their taxes. Now, in your case, this was set up at a bank in Pensacola. There weren't many banks in Florida in those days, and fortunately, the one the general chose was bought up by other banks over the years and is still in existence."

"So the bank in Pensacola has been taking money from the trust to pay the taxes all these years?" I asked.

"Yes," the young lawyer said. He paused for a moment to wipe his forehead with a monogrammed handkerchief. "I believe the deed in Mr. Darryl Norwood's custody must be a fake," he added. "I'm not sure where he got it, and I'm not sure it matters to us. If it's fabricated and he knows it, he could face criminal charges, but that's beyond what I think we should be focused on here."

"Well, then, what are we focused on here?" Dolores asked suspiciously.

"Producing your deed in court and stopping Darryl Norwood's development in its tracks."

Dolores grinned. "Ain't you some young whippersnapper?" she asked, causing him to blush flamingo pink from the base of his neck to his forehead. "Well," she added, "that's what I want. It's only right. The way I was raised, land is the greatest wealth a person can have, other than family. There's just one problem."

"What's that?" Mr. Yonce asked nervously.

"I can't pay you for all this work you're doing," she said. "I'm land rich but cash poor. Unless I can get my hands on some of that money in the trust. But something tells me that money's tied up in a neat little knot. Or else it wouldn't be there no more."

"You are correct," Mr. Yonce said. "We can look into it but I rather doubt you have access to it. The money is there to pay the taxes year after year, just to be sure it stays in the family."

"Dolores," I interrupted, "your friends are going to pay Mr. Yonce."

"What friends?"

"Dolores, I thought I told you before. If we needed to hire a lawyer, Mrs. Bailey White, Plain Jane, and Jackie Hart are going to pay for it. If I had any money, I would chip in, too."

"What about your son?" Mr. Yonce asked Dolores. He shuffled through his notes. "Robbie-Lee Simpson, lives in New York City. Works as an usher at a theater."

"What about him?" Dolores said icily.

"Can he help you? I mean financially? Have you spoken to him?"

Dolores sighed. "I get letters from him. He's been gone over a year now, but I don't want him to think I need him."

"But Dolores," I said gently, "the fact is you do need him."

"He needs to be brought into the picture

if for no other reason than he is your heir," Mr. Yonce said.

"I hadn't thought of it like that," Dolores said so softly I barely heard her. "Go ahead," she added. "Just do what you got to do."

Mr. Yonce asked a few other questions. Had she ever had a driver's license? A Social Security card? Was there a birth certificate, other than the one filled out by a midwife?

She said no to the remainder of his questions, but I had a feeling that her mind was now far away.

TWENTY-SIX

Our young lawyer, bless his city-born heart, was turning out to be a real go-getter. He called Jackie the following afternoon with big news: He had persuaded a Collier County judge to sign a stop-work order on Darryl's project until a hearing could be held.

The only downside was that the judge wanted the hearing to take place the following Wednesday, which did not give us much time, Jackie said.

Time for what? I wondered to myself. I'd left Mississippi during the last week of August. It was now early November. From my way of thinking, the sooner this whole thing was over, the better. But there were several details that Mr. Yonce needed to nail down.

Jackie explained it to us over tea sandwiches prepared by Mrs. Bailey White. "He said he has to hire a genealogist to verify

278

that Dolores — er, Bunny — is in fact a descendant of the general," she said. "He knows a professional who could do the work pronto."

"What if there are other descendants?" Plain Jane asked.

"Good question!" Jackie said. "Actually, even if there are others it only takes one descendant to step forward and file a stop-work order and have a chance to prove that Darryl is not the owner of the property. If there are other descendants, well, they can sort out what they want to do — or not do — with the property later. It's not relevant now."

"Jackie, you are starting to sound like a lawyer," Plain Jane teased.

"Well, I talked to Mr. Yonce on the phone for an hour, and he was pretty good about explaining things to me. You know, I always wanted to be a lawyer. I mean, if I had a profession, that's what I —"

"What else did he say?" I interrupted.

"Oh," Jackie said, flustered. "Let's see. There is a copy of the deed at the bank in Pensacola. The fact that Dolores — uh, *Bunny* — has the original deed is very important. Possession is nine-tenths of the law."

"There's something I'm wondering

about," I said. Even I could hear the anxiety in my voice. "I hate to say this, but even if the genealogist shows that Bunny Ann McIntyre is a direct descendant of the general, how do we know for sure that she is, in fact, the real Bunny Ann McIntyre?"

"I thought of that, too," Plain Jane said, speaking quickly. "She says she's Bunny Ann McIntyre but she's been using the name Dolores Simpson for a long time. Darryl's lawyers could claim she's not the real Bunny. We need some additional proof. Do we have it?"

We all started talking at once, just like in our old book club days. "Girls, girls, one at a time!" Mrs. Bailey White said. "Dora, you first."

"Well, when I took Mr. Yonce to meet with her, he asked if she'd ever had a driver's license or a Social Security card and she said no. He also asked if she had a copy of her birth certificate other than the one we've all seen already — the one written up by a midwife. Again — no."

"What about a family Bible?" Mrs. Bailey White asked.

"Yes," I said, "she said there was one and her name was written in it, but she doesn't know where it is now."

"Excuse me, could I get a word in edgewise here?" Jackie asked crossly. She pushed a dangling lock of hair out of her eyes. "I already talked to Mr. Yonce about all this!"

"And what did he say?" Plain Jane said.

"He said this was all fine and good, but that it would be very helpful if we could prove she'd ever used the name Bunny Ann McIntyre."

"How are we going to do that?" Mrs. Bailey White said, dejected.

"Well, ideally, if we had some sort of identification from her younger days, especially if there was a photograph or, even better, fingerprints. Mr. Yonce said she could be fingerprinted again today and if it were a match, then there would be no question."

"Good Lord," Mrs. Bailey White said. "We better hope she was arrested somewhere along the line."

Jackie smiled in a wry sort of way. "Funny," she said, "that's exactly what our lawyer said."

"Maybe it's time we checked in with Robbie-Lee," Plain Jane said. "He might know."

"I wonder how he's doing way up thar in New York City," Mrs. Bailey White said, making it sound as if he were on a dangerous expedition to the North Pole. "I mean, I wonder if he's got himself any friends."

"He sounds pretty good in his letters," I said.

"Yes, but do you think he has a *special friend*?" Jackie asked hopefully. Robbie-Lee was what my mama's generation called "a doll" — handsome, charming, debonair, and absolutely useless in the romance department. He wasn't interested in women in the Biblical sense, but he was kind and respectful, and awfully fun to have around.

"I have no idea," I said. "I just hope he isn't lonely."

That evening, with our blessings, Jackie began trying to reach Robbie-Lee by telephone. I wish we had included him sooner. After all, this whole mess concerned his mother. But now our lawyer, Mr. Yonce, said it couldn't wait.

Jackie had some trouble reaching Robbie-Lee. The long-distance operator said there was no telephone at the address of the apartment where he lived — not too surprising, since having a phone was expensive and Robbie-Lee was pinching pennies. Jackie finally called the Booth Theatre on Broadway where Robbie-Lee worked as an usher and, after persuading one of the box-office ladies that this was a family emergency, a message was left for Robbie-Lee to call her collect on his break.

He called back within an hour, Jackie said, and was completely frantic. Jackie explained what was going on, as rapidly as she could. He was relieved, she told us, that nothing terrible had happened to his mother — he was sure that's why Jackie had called — but he was furious about Darryl's plans, the first he'd heard of them.

When Jackie told him about the deed, she couldn't judge his reaction. If he was surprised, it wasn't obvious. Then she told him the court date — just one week away — and asked if there was any chance he could come.

"By the way," she asked before they got off the phone, "would you happen to know if, well, if your mother has ever been arrested? It would take too long to explain right now but it would help us prove her case."

There was a long pause, Jackie said, and then he replied, "Yes, I think she was. A long time ago, before I was born. When she was working as a, um, dancer in Tampa." Then he added, "Listen, Jackie, I have to get back to work now."

She said it was hard to tell if that were really true.

TWENTY-SEVEN

While Mr. Yonce scoured the arrest records up in Hillsborough County, we tried to keep our minds occupied. We tried various things to distract us, including a picnic on the beach, an excursion to the library, and then a cookout where we got a little tipsy on account of Mrs. Bailey White making Jell-O wine.

Then Plain Jane got this idea that we should revive our book club, just for the time being. I was eager to participate. Working at the library in Jackson meant I'd been reading all the latest books as they came in. I read anything and everything. I was impatiently awaiting Hemingway's latest, *A Moveable Feast,* which was coming in December, and I'd just finished an unusual autobiographical novel by a young woman with schizophrenia called *I Never Promised You a Rose Garden.*

"What books have you read lately?" I

asked breathlessly.

"Ha! Funny you should ask," Plain Jane replied. I noticed everyone turned to look at Jackie.

"What?" Jackie asked. "Oh, I know what you mean. That book, *Tropic of Cancer.* Are you familiar with it, Dora? A novel, written by Henry Miller and published in France in the '30s. Apparently, considered too vulgar for Americans."

"That's because it *is* vulgar!" Mrs. Bailey White almost shouted.

"Well, let's just say that some of it is not in good taste," Plain Jane said. By way of explanation to me, she added, "It was finally published in the U.S. a few years ago and then the courts said it was obscene. I think it's available again now. Anyway, Jackie got her hands on a copy. Jackie, how did you get it, anyway?"

Jackie lit a cigarette. "I didn't buy it at the Book Nook, that's for sure."

"We read passages of it aloud, and it was shocking!" Mrs. Bailey White howled.

"Oh, I was just trying to get us out of the rut we were in."

"What rut was that?" Plain Jane asked.

"Reading books that were too safe."

"What else did you read?" I asked.

"Well, just before you came home we'd

285

been discussing *Cross Creek* by Marjorie Kinnan Rawlings," Plain Jane said.

"Oh, I read that in high school and liked it very much," I said, thrilled that we were now on safer ground. If only Priscilla, Robbie-Lee, and the librarian, Miss Lansbury, were here, it might feel like old times.

"I don't know why we read that," Jackie grumbled. "I really didn't care for it that much."

"She's the same author who wrote *The Yearling,*" Plain Jane replied testily, "and we all loved that."

"I liked that it was by a *woman* author and it's about Florida," said Mrs. Bailey White.

"I remember it as a pioneer story," I said, "except that instead of out west it was set in north-central Florida. It's a memoir, right? And she's very independent and endures all kinds of hardships —"

"Hardships?! She was out of her mind!" Jackie interrupted. "Poison ivy? Snakes? I could hardly read it. Why put yourself through something like that?"

"Oh, Jackie, you're missing the point!" Plain Jane said crossly, having stood and retrieved the book from Mrs. Bailey White's shelf. "Listen to this passage: 'It is more important to live the life one wishes to live, and to go down with it if necessary, quite contentedly, than to live more profitably but less happily.' "

"I agree, that is a beautiful sentiment," Jackie said snippily, "but I have never really understood this type of adventure memoir — you know, where some naïve person goes out into the wilderness and goes through all kinds of hell of their own making and somehow supposedly emerges as a better, fuller human being. *Ugh!*"

"Jackie, you have no spirit of adventure!" cried Plain Jane.

"How can you say that?" Jackie blew a stream of cigarette smoke toward the ceiling. "I live here, don't I? I came all the way from Boston to Collier County, doesn't that count for something? Why do we always end up talking about me, anyway? Let's talk about something else." She turned to me and, without blinking an eye, said, "Dora, speaking of *adventure,* when are you going to tell us what happened in Mississippi?"

Now if there is one thing I hate, it's being ambushed. I had been planning on telling them in my own good time.

"Jackie, must you always put Dora on the spot?" Plain Jane scolded.

"Oh, it's all right," I said, sighing. "I guess now's as good a time as any. Especially since

— as I keep telling y'all — I have to go back soon."

"Well, maybe you could start by telling us what Jackson, Mississippi, is like," Jackie prompted. "They certainly have been in the national news, lately —"

"Yes," I said, "that poor man, Medgar Evers! That was two months before I arrived in Jackson. The Klan is crazy there. I mean, killing a leader of the NAACP! In his own front yard. Right out in the open!"

"Did you see any protests, or altercations, or anything of that sort?" Plain Jane asked.

"You can't help but encounter some of it," I replied.

"But what's it like to be there — in the city, I mean?" Jackie persisted.

"Well, it's hard to describe, but there's a feeling like there's not enough air to breathe," I said, struggling to find the right words. "I guess it's like — well, like when a big summer storm is rolling in from the Gulf and you can see the lightning strikes on the horizon. The air is so ripe with electricity and humidity that it makes you shiver even though it's hot. Well, that's what Jackson feels like to me these days. Especially since those three civil rights workers were murdered in June in that little city over in Neshoba County."

"You mean the city they call Philadelphia, of all things," Jackie said.

"Yes," I said.

"Well, I guess that's the difference between Mississippi and here," Plain Jane said. "Florida is still waking up."

"Actually, I think we are in the land of *Rip Van Winkle,*" Jackie said sarcastically. "In twenty years' time we'll wake up and discover that the civil rights movement has arrived here."

"Maybe not!" I said. "I mean, maybe sooner than that. I can't believe I forgot to tell you about the speaker I heard over at the Methodist church. I wish you all had been there. She was from some place in Ohio. An activist, I guess. She said we were ten years behind Mississippi, Alabama, and Georgia."

"No surprise there," Jackie said.

"But don't you see?" I asked. "A year ago that lady activist from Ohio wouldn't have been invited to speak here. *She was right here in Naples at one of the Methodist churches.* Isn't that progress?"

"Yes, I suppose it is," said Jackie. I must have looked skeptical because she added, "I mean it seriously. I agree with you, Dora."

"I think Florida is more genteel," Mrs. Bailey White said. "Yes, we have the Klan, but they're just a bunch of idiots running around in the bushes setting churches on fire. Things like the Medgar Evers assassination — that doesn't happen in Florida."

"Oh, yes it does!" Jackie said. "What about that man, Harry Moore, and his wife? The Klan put dynamite under their house and killed them on Christmas Day back in 1951 in some little town in Brevard County."

"Why, Jackie, you've been doing your homework," Plain Jane said admiringly.

"Well, there is some information at the library," Jackie said. "But Ted's been doing research when he's been traveling around the state. He even went to the NAACP office in Tampa and picked up some pamphlets there."

"Y'all are going to get yourselves shot!" Mrs. Bailey White said. "Mercy!"

"Well, Ted and I feel that we should try to understand what is happening, and the only way you can know that is to study the situation," Jackie said.

"Oh boy," Plain Jane remarked under her breath.

"What is that supposed to mean, Jane?" Jackie seemed surprised.

"It means that you're a typical Yankee," Mrs. Bailey White said. "You think you can solve every problem by studying it to death and asking questions. *Ha, ha, ha.*"

"Let's get back to Dora and her stay in Mississippi," Jackie snapped. "Did you ever feel like you were in danger?"

"In danger of what?" I asked, taken aback. "It's the black people who are in danger. Plus, the few white people who are trying to help them."

"So you didn't try to help the black people?" Jackie asked. She seemed disappointed.

"How?" I asked. "I'm from Florida. I don't understand Mississippi. I don't think I should presume to tell them how to fix their problems. I might have made things worse."

"But you might have made things *better,*" Jackie said softly.

Mrs. Bailey White spoke up again. "Now, don't admonish Dora. That's not why she went to Mississippi. She is still grieving her mama's death and went there to look for her people. She did her part. Besides, it ain't Dora's job to fix the world!"

"Well!" Jackie said furiously. "That's so . . . *Southern!* Mind your own business, pass the buck . . ."

"Jackie," I said grimly, "I'm doing my part in my own way. For instance, every Tuesday my landlady Mrs. Conroy and I cook dinner for the black leaders."

"What?" Jackie said. "What do you mean?"

I wondered how much I should share with them, even though they were my closest friends. I remembered that old World War Two saying "Loose lips sink ships." "Well," I began slowly, "y'all have to promise me that this doesn't go beyond this room. But there is concern that someone may try to, er, harm the leaders, like the Rev. Martin Luther King when he comes to town."

Jackie quickly put two and two together. "You mean *poison*?" she asked, aghast.

"Sure," I said, "among other ways. I don't know what they have in place to protect him from being shot or anything like that. I'm sure there must be bodyguards. But somebody figured out that the food he and the other leaders eat could be tampered with. So the way it works is there's a very small group of people like me and Mrs. Conroy who volunteer to cook at home using ingredients we buy or grow. This is all very hush-hush, of course. We prepare the food and pretend we're taking it to Mrs. Conroy's church for potluck night. But instead the food is picked up by a Negro janitor at Mrs. Conroy's church. He gives it that same day to his colored preacher, who takes it directly to the colored side of town himself."

"My goodness!" Jackie said, "who dreamed this up?"

"I have no idea," I replied.

"Wait — Mrs. Conroy is involved? Isn't that the same lady you said was nervous as a rat terrier?" Plain Jane asked.

"Well, she is," I said, blushing a little at my unkind characterization. "She also has a heart of gold. And she belongs to one of the white churches that is trying to help the Negroes."

"Never mind all that, have you actually met Dr. King?" Jackie asked, wide-eyed.

"No," I said. "But I know I helped feed him whenever he was in Jackson."

"Oh, Dora, I am so proud of you," Mrs. Bailey White gushed.

"What else did you do?" Plain Jane asked.

I paused and thought about it. "I noticed in Jackson that I hadn't seen any groups like our book club — you know, white people who welcomed a black person to join," I said. "I don't see that kind of social-izing go on between the races there at all. So every time I meet a new person in Jack-son, I find a way to tell them all about our Priscilla and how smart she is, that we were in a book club together and now she's studying at Bethune-Cookman College."

"How is that supposed to change things?" Jackie asked.

"Are you kidding? That's the best way to make change happen!" Plain Jane cried. "By pointing out that she is friends with a black person, and that the black person is someone she likes and admires!"

"Oh, brother," Jackie said. "If that's progress, it'll only take a hundred years."

There was enough tension in the air to fry a rabbit so we went to our separate corners. Mrs. Bailey White made some kind of excuse and disappeared into her kitchen, where she puttered about doing this and that; Plain Jane attended to the baby (we could hear her cooing, her voice echoing in high pitches down the staircase); Jackie went outside to clean the windshield of her car and have a smoke; and I went into Mrs. Bailey White's paneled library. Studying her books, taking them down one by one, was soothing. What is it about books? They are like old friends.

About an hour later, Mrs. Bailey White rounded us up like she was Mother Goose and we, her little goslings. She asked that we return to the parlor. Once there, she announced, "Now, girls, let's focus on Dora, and what she learned about her family, if anything, on her trip." To me, she said kindly, "Take your time, dear."

I cleared my throat. "Well," I began slowly, "as you know, I always wondered why I was named after a well-known writer from Mississippi, and figured Mama may have been friends with Eudora Welty, or maybe even kinfolk. Or maybe Mama had just been an admirer. But I realized that the first thing I should do is read all of her books. Miss Welty's, I mean. I read *The Robber Bridegroom* on the bus on the way to Mississippi. Once I got settled I read everything I could get my hands on. And frankly it made me a little uneasy. Because Miss Welty's writing is a little off-putting at times. Intimidating."

"Well, that one is especially eerie," Plain Jane interjected. "Sorry. I didn't mean to interrupt."

"So anyway I read them all," I continued, "just because I thought it would be rude not to. I mean, who goes to visit a famous writer and hasn't read her books? I wasn't even sure I would get to talk to her, but it seemed respectful to be prepared.

"All this time I was working up my nerve. Finally, I decided that I was being a ninny. What was the worst thing that could happen? That she would turn me away? Everyone in town knew where she lived, so I went over there on the bus and walked back and forth on the sidewalk trying to work up my nerve. Then I realized Mama would not approve of me, a complete stranger, just knocking on Miss Welty's door. So I went back to Mrs. Conroy's and wrote a letter. I told Miss Welty that I was living in town temporarily to find out more about my late mother, whose name was Callie Francine Atwater of the Jackson Atwaters, and that Callie had married a man named Montgomery Witherspoon, known to all as Monty, and that I was their only child. And that I wouldn't be bothering her — with her being an important writer and all — except I believed she may have known my mother at one time, and that in fact my name is Eudora Welty Witherspoon and while it could be a coincidence it seems highly unlikely in my most humble opinion. So I wrote this in a letter. And I mailed it.

"Of course, I hoped (and truth be told, prayed) that I would hear back from her if for no other reason than to clear up the mystery of my name. Three days later I received a letter. When I came home from my job at the library, Mrs. Conroy was standing on the porch waiting for me. The mailman had just been there. I'm still amazed Mrs. Conroy didn't steam it open because she can be nosy as a raccoon and not half as subtle, bless her heart.

"I went upstairs to open it. It was an invitation from Miss Welty to visit her at her home the following Sunday afternoon at three o'clock. That was all. Just a handwritten note, one sentence long.

"I was relieved and happy that she'd replied but as the days passed — slow as molasses, it seemed to me — I started dreading what she might tell me. I'm not sure why. I was prepared for her to say almost anything.

"Finally, Sunday arrived, and after church and Sunday dinner with Mrs. Conroy, it was time to go. I was so scared I'd be late that I got to Miss Welty's neighborhood a half-hour early. At five minutes till three, I knocked on her door. She answered herself. She's a plain little thing, but the type of person who has presence.

" 'Do you mind if we sit in the garden?' she asked me. 'My mother is upstairs and feeling very poorly today.'

"And of course I said I was sorry to hear that, but the garden would be fine. So we sat in her garden — oh, what a garden! — and —"

"Wait — she has a lovely garden?" Mrs. Bailey White interrupted. Mrs. Bailey White had what Mama used to call "garden envy." Some folks have kitchen envy, some have porch envy. Mrs. Bailey White salivated over lush flower gardens.

"Let's not talk about that now —" Jackie said.

"Does she have climbing roses?" Mrs. Bailey White persisted. "I just love climbing roses."

"Why, yes, Mrs. Bailey White, she does! She has Lady Banks, American Beauty, Mermaid, and some others I didn't recognize."

"Oh, I wish I could see it!" Mrs. Bailey White said plaintively.

"Mrs. Bailey White, we all love gardens," Plain Jane said gently, "but let's let Dora get back to her story."

"Well," I continued, "we talked about her books until finally she broached the subject by saying, 'I was sad to learn from your letter that your mother has died.'

"Well, it all came tumbling out of her — this story from before I was born. Mama and Miss Welty had been friends in school, with both pledging they would remain independent, unmarried and childless, and pursue careers as writers.

"I never saw Mama write anything more than a grocery list. But Miss Welty said

Mama had been a 'grand writer' with 'a lot of promise.' Then she said with a smile that Mama had been a 'great beauty' who 'had everything a person could dream of.'

"She went on to say that Mama was 'the belle of the ball,' from a rich family, and then one day she turned everything upside-down: She ran away on the day of her wedding in 1931."

"She *what*?" Mrs. Bailey White shrieked.

"She left her betrothed at the altar. And she took off with my daddy instead." It was hard to push those words out of my mouth. But I did.

"How exciting!" Jackie declared, and lit another cigarette.

"Good heavens, Dora," Plain Jane said sympathetically. "That's a lot to think about."

"Well, I had no idea that Mama was ever engaged to someone other than Daddy. She always seemed like such a sensible person. I couldn't imagine her leaving a man at the altar, abandoning her family and friends, and disappearing. That's not the woman I knew my whole life."

"I'm sorry, Dora," Jackie said, furrowing her brow. "I didn't mean to make light of it."

"Did Miss Welty tell you anything else?"

Plain Jane asked gently.

"Well, I asked if she was there when Mama . . . well, when all that happened at the church, and she said, no, she missed the whole drama on account of it happened at the same time her daddy took sick and died from leukemia."

"Oh, that's sad," Mrs. Bailey White said. "What else did she say?"

"Well, I asked her, 'Are Mama's parents still living?' and 'Did Mama have any brothers or sisters?'"

"Her answer, to both, was no. And I have to tell you, I was very disappointed. Somehow I had pictured Mama having a brother or sister. I would have loved having an aunt or uncle, or cousins. And another thing — Miss Welty was surprised to hear that Mama remained a nurse. She said, 'I thought she was doing that just because her parents told her not to. I didn't realize she stayed with it. Maybe it was her true calling.' And then Miss Welty looked straight at me and with no warning at all, she said, 'Well, Miss Witherspoon, what is *your* calling?'"

"And that's when I told her about you — the Book Club, I mean — and how y'all have told me that you think I have a knack for storytelling. And while I didn't know if I had what it takes to make a living as a writer, I had been trying my hand at it."

"Did she read anything you wrote?" Jackie interrupted.

"Why, yes, she did," I said. "She asked me to come back a week later and bring something I'd written."

"Wow," Jackie said, "and then what happened?"

"Oh, let Dora tell the story!" Plain Jane said.

"That's right," Mrs. Bailey White said. "Just let her tell it."

They all stared at me with excitement.

"Well," I said slowly, "I brought her a short story and she read it."

"But what did she *say*?" Jackie persisted.

"Do you want the truth?" I asked.

"Of course we want the truth," Jackie said uneasily.

I thought it best to blurt it out. "She said it wasn't authentic."

"Authentic?!" Mrs. Bailey White cried out. "What is that supposed to mean?"

My friends looked wounded, as indeed I had been at the time, until I admitted a simple truth to myself: Miss Welty was right.

"What it means is that I was trying too hard to write about something I didn't know anything about."

"Well, what did you write about?" Plain

Jane asked.

"A short story about a girl who has a love affair in Paris," I replied.

"But you've never been to Paris," Jackie said, stating the obvious.

"Miss Welty said the same thing," I said. "She said it's possible to write about a place you've never been but you shouldn't 'undervalue' your own experiences. She said something about Paris being overdone."

"I don't see how Paris could ever be *overdone,*" Jackie said.

"I think she meant, *written about too often,* when there are other places that no one ever seems to write about," I said. "She said that if I wrote about a love affair in Paris, maybe, at least, one of the characters could be visiting from Collier County, just to make it fresh."

"Ah, I see," Plain Jane said approvingly.

"This will sound funny," I added. "On my way back to my landlady's house a phrase kept popping into my head. I don't know where it came from. Maybe from Mama in the Spirit World. It was, *Listen to your own stories.*"

"Oh," Jackie said. "I like that!"

"So you're going to keep writing, right, Dora?" Plain Jane asked. "Because we think you should, don't we?" Jackie and Mrs.

Bailey White nodded in agreement.

"I'll tell you what, Dora, the part about your mother running off with another man on her wedding day — *ooooWEE,* that must have been something," Mrs. Bailey White said.

"Now there's a story for you to tell," Jackie added.

I felt something closing around my heart, like a protective shield, much like a turtle, I thought, as it withdraws into its shell. There was more to say but I was not ready to tell the rest.

TWENTY-EIGHT

This is what I kept to myself.

After my two meetings with Miss Welty, I did some research on my lunch hour at the library. I looked through old copies of the *Clarion-Ledger,* looking for stories about Mama.

I could have done this when I first came to Jackson, but I didn't. I guess I just wasn't ready then.

I worked my way through each massive index of the newspaper for the time frame Mama lived in Jackson, checking for her name year after year until I found three separate news stories in which she was said to be mentioned. I filled out a microfilm request, trying to look nonchalant while the staff at the research desk went to look for them. The rolls of microfilm, once they were retrieved, had to be threaded into a machine in order to read them, a difficult task when your hands are trembling.

I scrolled too fast and had to back up the machine to see the first news story. Suddenly there she was, Miss Callie Francine Atwater, along with Miss Eudora Welty, in a news photograph of the two of them sharing a prize for a spelling bee. Miss Welty hadn't mentioned that. Perhaps it wasn't important.

More shocking was seeing Mama in the social pages as a debutante at a cotillion, looking fancy in a special gown ordered from a store in New York City called Bergdorf Goodman's, according to the article. I stared at the photograph. No question about it. This was my mama. The same person who never spent money on clothes and hadn't seemed to care about fashion one bit.

Then I found the wedding announcement. MISS ATWATER TO MARRY MR. JENKINS TODAY IN GREENWOOD, said the headline. I could scarcely breathe as I read the story. "Miss Callie Francine Atwater, daughter of local bank president James T. Atwater and his wife, Jane, is to be married at 11 o'clock today to Mr. Harold Jenkins of Lake Charles, Louisiana . . ." How strange to be reading the announcement of a wedding that never came to be. The article went on to describe her dress and mentioned a bridesmaid, Miss Alice B. Johnson.

I felt someone's presence behind me, a little shadow over my right shoulder. It was the head librarian, Mrs. LaCroix. "I see you're digging up the past," she said, trying, but failing, to sound lighthearted. She spoke in a soft, hushed tone out of respect for the silence-only rule which librarians alone were allowed to break, and only in the quietest murmurs. "I wondered how long before you'd start looking in these old newspapers. Ah," she added, "I see you've found the society pages."

"Did you know my mother?" I asked pointedly — and a little too loud. When I'd been interviewed for my job, I'd mentioned that Mama grew up in Jackson. When I said Mama's name at the time, several of the librarians — including Mrs. LaCroix — had acted a little funny but I wasn't sure if it meant anything.

"Everyone knew your mother, dear," she whispered. "She was the star of her generation around here."

"And do you know what happened to her?"

Mrs. LaCroix looked at me, surprised. "Don't you?"

"I only know that she didn't marry this man," I said, trying to keep my voice low and pointing to the microfilm page with the account of the wedding. "On that same day she married my daddy, whose name was Montgomery Witherspoon, and they went to Florida, where Daddy was from, and they had me." My mind was spinning like a little wind-up toy Mama had given me as a child and which I still had, despite the fact that it was broken. "What has happened to Mr. Harold Jenkins?" I asked. "Do you know?"

Mrs. LaCroix pulled up a chair and sat next to me. "He died in the war," she said. "After what happened — with your mama and all — he had a broken heart and went back to Louisiana. That's what I've heard for years. And even though he was a little old to serve in World War Two, he enlisted. And he was killed. I'm not sure when or where. We could look that up if you want to. Or I could write to the librarian in Lake Charles . . ."

"It seems like everyone is dead," I said sadly. "Everyone who could give me real answers, anyway."

"Not everyone has passed away," Mrs. La-Croix said. "The bridesmaid. She's sitting right over there."

I jerked my head in the direction Mrs. La-Croix was pointing. A gray-haired lady sat half hidden behind a broadsheet newspaper.

I had noticed her before. She was what we called a "regular."

The next thing I knew I was being introduced, in library-appropriate hushed tones, to my mother's long-ago bridesmaid. While I could not have been more surprised, she seemed to have been expecting this moment to occur. Perhaps, I realized, even waiting for the right moment to speak to me, these last several months.

Miss Alice B. Johnson was a lifelong Jackson resident from a neighborhood I recognized as a poor white part of town. She had never married, she said, and still lived at home with her mother. To support herself, she worked nights as a telephone operator.

"Call me Miss Alice," she said warmly. Aware that we were creating a small disruption, and that we had definitely abused the silence-only rule, we agreed to duck outside for a little stroll. My lunch hour had elapsed, but Mrs. LaCroix nodded her approval and smiled encouragingly.

The sidewalk was sun dappled and welcoming but too crowded with children walking home from school to hold a private conversation. I did not want to miss a word. Miss Alice gestured to a side street that was blessedly empty of activity except for a small dog sniffing at the base of a magnolia tree. We found a little bench where we could talk quietly.

"Your mama wanted to be just like us," Miss Alice said.

"Like who?" I asked.

Miss Alice surprised me by chuckling. "Like down-to-earth folks. Ordinary people who didn't put on airs. She and I met over at the Salvation Army. The only difference was, she was a volunteer and I was a client. But we were the same age and we became friends. She confided in me. When she asked me to be her only bridesmaid, I didn't know what to do. I couldn't afford the dress. But she said, 'Don't worry about it, I'll pay for it.' Then I started worrying that maybe her parents wouldn't want me in the wedding. It was during the Depression, but your grandpa was still a wealthy man or at least that's the impression he gave. And your grandma was active in the Episcopal Church, which is for upper-class folk, you know. But your mama said, 'Oh, don't worry. It's my wedding, and I want you in it.'"

"Did you know that Mama was going to run off with someone else?" The words were painful to say.

"I knew she was in love with someone else

but I wasn't privy to her plans," Miss Alice said tactfully. "Or maybe there were no plans. Maybe she just up and did it."

I was having a hard time picturing Mama being so impulsive, and Miss Alice read my mind. "She was young," she said. "We were all very young. People do things they'd never do when they're older. And sometimes it's impossible to look back and understand.

"What your mama really wanted," she added, "was to be just plain folk. She didn't want nothin' to do with the highfalutin family she was born into. She even learned to talk like me. And she surely didn't want to marry that fellow from Louisiana. That wasn't her dream. Her dream was to be a nurse among the downtrodden. She was going to give up all her fancy airs. And then somehow — maybe at the Salvation Army — she ran into your daddy, Montgomery Witherspoon. Oh, he was a bad boy. Had been in jail and everything. But I think she saw in him a way for all of her dreams to come true: A simple life. Helping others." She thought for a moment and added, "He was her way out."

"Daddy had been in *jail*?" I choked on the word.

"Yes'm, but I don't know what for. Nothing too terrible or I'd remember that. Where is he, do you know?"

"No," I said, "I don't know what happened to him. All I know is Mama said there was a big fuss when I was a baby, and Daddy up and left. I believe he's dead. When I was growing up, Mama gave folks the impression she was a widow but come to think of it, I never actually heard her use that word. Maybe implying that he was dead was her way of keeping up appearances. It's a lot easier to be a widow than a divorcée in this world, that's for sure. Anyway, whatever happened between them didn't end well. I always had the feeling she was embarrassed by him, or something he'd done."

"Maybe he was prone to drinkin'," Miss Alice said sympathetically. "Lots of menfolk are."

"Miss Alice," I said, desperate to put more pieces together. "Have you been watching me? Or is it a coincidence that you come to the library all the time? How did you know who I am?"

She smiled a little mischievously. "A little bird told me that a gal calling herself Eudora Welty Witherspoon was in town, and that her mama had been Miss Callie Atwater. And I thought, *Now that's mighty peculiar.* I thought maybe the Lord hisself wants me to find out what this is all about.

Maybe to help you in some way since your mama and I were friends back in the day."

"But how —"

"Child, Jackson may seem like a big city to you but it's a small town at heart. My mother took a Bible study class with your landlady, Mrs. Conroy. And one day Mrs. Conroy mentioned she had a gal staying with her, and she said your name and that you were working at the library. My mother told me, and that's all I needed to know."

"Well, I am grateful to you," I said. "I thank you for telling me what you know."

It was the wrong thing to say. She looked away, and a deep uneasiness swept through me.

"There's something else," she said finally. When she glanced back at me, her smile was gone and her face sagged, making her look much older. "What your mama really wanted most was a child, but I was pretty sure she couldn't have one." She looked at me closely, as if studying my features, then said, "Maybe I shouldn't be telling you all this, but it seems wrong that you don't know. The fact is your mama had some kind of fever that almost killed her when she was, oh, maybe sixteen. And after that, she was told she'd never be able to have children."

"So you're saying I was a surprise?" I said,

but the second the words left my lips I realized she meant something else entirely. "Do you think . . . ? Are you saying — ?"

"— that you might have been adopted?" Miss Alice said softly. "Could be." She paused a moment, then added, "Then again, maybe you're some kind of miracle baby." She tried her best to smile brightly, but I don't think she was convinced. And neither was I.

Finding out that you might be adopted is one thing. Finding out at the age of thirty-two, and from a person you've known for exactly ten minutes, is a tough row to hoe.

"Mama always said I was born in Naples, at home," I said quietly. "I suppose that might not be true."

"Well, what does your birth certificate say?"

"I don't have one."

"Everyone has one."

"No, Mama said she never got around to registering me. I found that out when I got married. Before we could get the marriage license, Mama had to swear in an affidavit that she was my mama and that I was born at home in Naples."

"I see," Miss Alice said.

What she could see, and so could I, was that it might all have been lies. And the worst part was not being able to ask Mama because she was dead. Just ask her; that's all I wanted. I would have accepted the idea of being adopted, if only she had told me herself.

I told Miss Alice a little about my life, what Naples was like, and about my failed marriage to Darryl. She asked what had led me to come to Jackson to find out about Mama, and I told her about the Collier County Women's Literary Society and how the founder, a newcomer to Naples named Jackie Hart, had encouraged me to get out in the world, ask questions, and experience life. I had known immediately that I should go to Jackson, if for no other reason than to see where Mama had come from. And then I told Miss Alice what Mama's life had been like in Naples, and how she'd gotten sick. And how she died.

Miss Alice listened carefully. "Well," she said finally, "I'm just glad she had you with her when she got sick." Then she turned directly to face me. There were tears in her eyes, but she smiled as she added, "I hope you realize that you must have meant the *world* to her, Dora. She was truly blessed. And so are you."

TWENTY-NINE

We had four days until the hearing at the Collier County Courthouse, and Mrs. Bailey White was beginning to fret. "I do believe that we should provide some new clothes and, um, a little *assistance* with Bunny's appearance for the court date," she said. "I know from my own experience, during my murder trial, that it's important to look your best."

I'm sure I flinched and I have little doubt the others did, too. I'd never been able to come to terms with Mrs. Bailey White's past — not fully anyway — but at the same time I was happy for the diversion. Any topic was preferable to the possibility that they would ask more questions about my discoveries in Mississippi.

"As a matter of fact, I'm glad you brought this up, Mrs. Bailey White," Jackie said, interrupting my thoughts. "I've been sitting here trying to figure out how we're going to get her into town for fingerprinting. Mr. Yonce said it was imperative. And I agree. We need to fix her up for court, if she lets us. Maybe we should, um, *retrieve* her from the, er, *swamp,* get these things done, then keep her in town — maybe just for one night — so that we can be sure she gets to court."

"She could stay here the night before," Mrs. Bailey White said thoughtfully. "I mean, if she's willing to."

"I have some clothes that might fit," Plain Jane interjected from across the room. "Or, at least, we can alter them. Maybe we should all ransack our closets and see what we can come up with."

And so it was agreed, at least by everyone except, of course, Bunny. Jackie even offered to pay for a trip to the hair salon and said she would escort Bunny there if I promised to go along for moral support. But someone had to get Bunny out of Gun Rack Village and into Naples. Jackie still refused to drive in Gun Rack Village, citing wear and tear on the convertible, and I balked at canoeing again. My hands were still sore from paddling Mr. Yonce over there and back. And I didn't feel like going on foot again, either.

I took a chance and left a note for her at

the Esso station. I knew that Billy and Marco, the pair of brothers who lived somewhere along the river, were in the habit of stopping by the Esso station almost daily. Bucky, who owned the gas station, was pretty reliable and agreed to give my note to them. Hopefully, the brothers would then deliver it to her.

The note was hard to write. How do you tell someone that she needs to get gussied up for court? That her hair and clothes won't do? That she needed to be finger-printed at the police department? That we wanted her to stay the night before court at Mrs. Bailey White's house because we didn't want to take any chances that she wouldn't show up?

I kept the note very short. This was one of those "the less said, the better" moments. If it didn't work, I'd have to hike back there and persuade her to return with me.

To my surprise, at precisely two o'clock the day before court, Bunny arrived at the Edge of Everglades House of Beauty, just as I'd hoped. Marco and Billy had not only re-trieved my note from Bucky and delivered it to her, they had saved her the long hike into town by giving her a ride.

This seemed like a minor miracle to Jackie

and me. We'd been nervously waiting at the beauty parlor, flipping randomly through magazines devoted to the latest hairstyles, none of which, to be honest, would look good on anyone we knew. The beauty salon's owner kept a radio tuned to WNOG, "Wonderful Naples on the Gulf." At one point Jackie turned to me and said, "Oh, for Pete's sake. If I hear that Beatles song 'I Want to Hold Your Hand' one more time, I might have a stroke and die. My kids play it day and night and I hear it everywhere I go."

"I like the Beatles," I said lamely.

"Do you know what Judd said?" Jackie asked. "He said the school principal at the junior high held an assembly and said just two words into the microphone — 'The Beatles' — and two girls screamed."

"Well, aren't girls everywhere screaming over the Beatles?" I asked.

"That's the point! It means that the cultural phenomenon known as the Beatles has even reached the end of the earth — that is, Naples."

We didn't even realize that Bunny was standing right in front of us, listening. She must have slipped through the door while we were having our Beatlemania discussion, which, judging by the look on her face, was all news to her. She sort of nodded and grunted something that might have been "hello."

The sight of Bunny sent a shock wave through the salon. The other women in the salon stopped talking abruptly. Their heads swiveled in unison. Even the ladies trapped under hair dryers were trying to get a good look.

Jackie was gracious. "So glad you could join us!" Her words of welcome were scarcely said when the owner of the beauty parlor scurried up to us. "What have we here?" she asked, with alarm.

"Of course you meant *whom* do we have here?" Jackie said sweetly. "This is the woman I was telling you about. As I mentioned before, it's my treat."

The hairdresser looked doubtful.

"I was thinking maybe a bouffant of some sort, though maybe she needs some color first," Jackie said, taking Bunny's arm and escorting her to the nearest washbasin.

Bunny actually half smiled at the other customers. "I would like a manicure, too," she announced, and, in one of those peculiar moments of perfect timing, a new Roy Orbison song called "Oh, Pretty Woman" started playing on the radio. To some people, it might have seemed like irony, but to

319

me it was like a little message of love or tip of the hat, meant just for her.

"Oh, I forgot to make introductions!" Jackie cried out. "Miss Bunny Sanders, please meet Miss Dolores Simpson. Actually, Dolores's name is Bunny, too, but I keep forgetting to call her that. Shame on me —"

"Bunny?!" The proprietor took a step back. *"Bunny?"* she repeated. "Her name cannot be Bunny. Apparently you have forgotten, Mrs. Hart, that *I am Bunny.*"

Jackie looked confused. "Oh," she said quickly, "two Bunnies! How cute! You know, I never knew anyone in Boston named Bunny but now I know *two* Bunnies."

Poor Jackie. She had failed to comprehend that here in the South it is a well-known fact that trouble can ensue when two gals in a small town have the same first name. Southern women are like a bee colony. They just can't tolerate two queens in one hive.

I cupped my hand and whispered a quick explanation into Jackie's ear. She looked at me like I had lost my mind. "What are you talking about?" she said a little too loud. "Why can't there be two Bunnies?"

You could fault men for all kinds of things, but no man, I felt sure, would have a problem with having the same first name as another. Why, I bet you could have a whole room full of Bobs and they'd probably just call themselves Bob 1, Bob 2, Bob 3, and so on. Or they'd just call each other by their last names. But you couldn't have two Bunnies in the little town of Naples.

For a moment I thought the hairdresser was going to ask us to leave. I could see she was mulling it over, but professional pride or Christian charity got the better of her. "We've got us some work to do!" she announced, in what was undoubtedly the understatement of the year. With remarkable speed she shampooed our Bunny's hair, slapped some goop on it, and led our Bunny to the only available hair dryer, which happened to be right smack in the middle of the row of all the others.

Bunny enjoyed being treated like a pampered swan. She even asked for a copy of *Screen Idol* magazine. *No doubt,* I thought, *to look for photos of Elizabeth Taylor.* Only when the manicurist was ready to do her nails — Bunny chose Petunia Pink — did she let go of the magazine.

As soon as the dryer was finished, Bunny the hairdresser rewashed our Bunny's hair, cut, and styled it. Jackie started to say something but did not; she was disappointed, I could tell, that her opinion on what she referred to as the *coiffure* was clearly unwelcome. This was not going as planned but it would have to be good enough. I was thankful when Jackie paid the bill and we could leave.

Bunny's new hairdo was a stunner: a mile-high tower of teased tresses reminiscent of cotton candy. Holding her hands so that her new manicure would finish drying, our Bunny did something I'm pretty sure she hadn't done in years: She smiled the type of full-faced grin that reminded me of a teen-age girl getting ready for prom.

As we left the shop, however, reality returned. "Bunny," I said, "I hate to ruin this Kodak moment, because we're having great fun here. Not to shanghai you or anything but there is something you need to know."

The smile vanished. "Go on," she said, jutting out her chin. Jackie, meanwhile, pretended to rummage in her purse for her car keys; by prearrangement, she was to stay silent during this part.

"Well, uh, it looks like it's got to come out in court that you were, um, arrested a long time ago," I said. "And it's actually a *good* thing because it means we have your finger-prints from when you were using the name Bunny Ann McIntyre. Now we can compare

322

them and prove that you are the same person. And Mr. Yonce says this will be necessary." I said this so rapidly even I wasn't sure what I'd just said.

Bunny simply shrugged. "Okay," she said. "But doesn't that mean we need to get some fresh fingerprints? We'd better get to it."

Here I had worried myself sick about this pending conversation, and yet Bunny had taken it in stride. She was definitely a more complex person than I had thought.

We walked to the sheriff's department, where our attorney Mr. Yonce was waiting for us. It was half past three on the day before court. We were cutting things very close.

With a desk sergeant acting as a witness, a deputy sheriff fingerprinted Bunny. Her only concern was that it had messed up her manicure.

As soon as the prints were dry, Mr. Yonce said they would be examined that night by a fingerprint expert. Our young lawyer certainly seemed to have everything under control, but before we left he whispered to me, "We better hope these are a perfect match. We might win anyway, but this would seal the deal."

There was one more task: figuring out what

Bunny was going to wear in court.

Once again, Bunny proved to be a surprisingly good sport. At Mrs. Bailey White's house we laid out all the possible outfits and let her choose. Jackie had brought a few things from her closet. Plain Jane had purchased some items at a church rummage sale, including gloves and a hat. Mrs. Bailey White offered costume jewelry and shoes. And my contribution was a small makeup kit I bought for half-price during a sale at the Rexall.

There was a risk of offending Bunny, of course, but there was another problem as well. None of us wanted to address the fact that Bunny's artificially enhanced bustline made her figure completely out of proportion.

Thankfully, Jackie anticipated the problem by creating what one might call a modified muumuu (although she described it as "reminiscent of what Liz Taylor might wear when she is entertaining at home"). Essentially, she had taken one of her own housecoats, added a little elastic here and there, altered the sleeves, and added a patent leather belt. The result was passably good. Bunny tried it on and seemed very pleased.

I had been worried about Bunny's reaction to the baby but when Plain Jane brought Dream into the room, Bunny sort of half smiled and nodded in Dream's direction in the way women do when they see a beautiful baby, even one that was the "wrong" color. For all I knew, Bunny might have balked at staying even one night under the same roof with a colored child, but she said nothing. The only thing left was for Bunny to have a good meal, a long hot soak in a bathtub (heaven only knows how long it had been), and a decent night's sleep in one of the guest rooms of Mrs. Bailey White's house.

Once Bunny was settled for the night, and Dream had drifted off to sleep, the rest of us convened for a nightcap of rose wine in the parlor. We talked over our plans for the next day when suddenly I blurted out that I had more to tell them about my visit to Jackson "if," I said, "y'all are in the mood to hear it."

"Of course we are in the mood to hear it," Jackie said. "If you feel like telling us now, by all means go ahead."

"Should I get us some warm milk?" Mrs. Bailey White asked.

"Forget the warm milk," Jackie said.

"Agreed," Plain Jane said, adding, "But thank you anyway."

"Can I just get this over with?" I said. I was tired and my nerves too raggedy to be as polite as I should have been. I took a deep breath while they focused their attention on me. "You know how I told you that I learned from Miss Welty that Mama had run off with Daddy on the day she was to marry someone else?" I said. "Well, there's more."

"Be brave, dear, what is it?" Plain Jane asked gently.

"I learned that I was almost certainly adopted," I said in a whisper, "and I doubt I'll ever find out what happened."

"What'd you say?" asked Mrs. Bailey White. "I can't hear you."

"She said she found out she was *adopted*," Plain Jane said loudly.

"Oh!" Mrs. Bailey White said. "I'm sorry I didn't hear you, please go on."

And so I told them the rest of the story, starting with what Miss Welty had said; about my research at the library; the newspaper stories on Mama; and meeting Miss Alice, Mama's long-ago bridesmaid. I explained how at first I felt like someone had died. I was in shock and grieving like when there's a tragedy. After that I was angry for a long while. I was so prickly I could have lost my job except my boss, the head librarian, felt sorry for me. For the first time in my life, I cussed often and over the littlest things, like dropping a nickel on the sidewalk and having to bend down to get it. That would just infuriate me. Everything seemed too much, like the world was out to get me in big ways and small. But I also laughed a lot, not because anything was funny but because of the irony of it. I had gone to Jackson to find out about Mama and, oh boy, I'd gotten a lot more information than I had bargained for.

Jackie, Plain Jane, and Mrs. Bailey White were listening carefully. After it was clear I was all talked out, Plain Jane spoke up. "You seem to be doing pretty well with this," she said gently.

"Well," I said, "I've had a few months to get used to the idea."

"Dora," Jackie said sympathetically. "If there's anything any of us can do —"

"Jackie, you make it sound like someone died," Plain Jane interrupted.

"Well, Dora herself said it felt like someone died," Jackie protested. "Oh, Dora, this really is terribly unfair, isn't it? I hope we will all see the day when people don't feel they have to be so secretive about adoption. It seems so much worse not to tell a child! I think if I had adopted any of my children I would have told them from the beginning."

"Well, that's not what the experts say," Plain Jane said solemnly. "I was just reading an article about it. It's better to wait until they're old enough to understand — or maybe never tell them at all. That's what it said."

"That's crazy," Jackie snapped. "Look at poor Dora here. I think the way she found out is the worst part."

"Ladies!" Mrs. Bailey White said. "Let us be thoughtful!" She gestured to me. I was sinking further and deeper into the seat cushions of the ancient sofa.

Plain Jane and Jackie rushed to apologize while Mrs. Bailey White poured me a teeny-tiny brandy and made me drink it. "Now, you listen to me, Miss Dora Witherspoon," she said firmly. "First, I want to say that you mustn't spend your life trying to find out more about the past. Some things are just meant to remain a mystery. Second, I don't know much about adoption but the woman you called 'Mama' loved you. She must have, because she raised you right. She's your real mother. The woman that's buried over yon in the Cemetery of Hope and Salvation. But since she won't have a chance to tell her side of this story — well, not until you meet her again in the Spirit

World — I think we shouldn't judge her."

I reached over and squeezed Mrs. Bailey White's hand, grateful for her wisdom.

THIRTY

The day of the court hearing dawned early for all of us. As agreed, Jackie picked me up at my cottage at six o'clock and we drove straight to Mrs. Bailey White's.

Jackie was nervous. She was dressed to the nines — still in mourning black but with a few extra flourishes like a heavy gold brooch and matching earrings that I'd never seen before.

"My mother's," she said, tugging gently on her earlobes when she saw me staring. "I want to look like I'm richer than I am," she added with a laugh. "We need to impress the judge."

I was wearing a light-gray suit with a lavender blouse. At least I had found some shoe polish and improved the appearance of my loafers. Well, if I could never pull off looking glamorous, at least I looked neat and presentable, but I made a silent promise that if I ever had any money to spare I would ask Jackie to take me shopping. Maybe even go to Miami or Palm Beach, though that was *really* dreaming on my part.

We arrived at the old house to find Mrs. Bailey White fluttering around like a bird that is trapped and trying to find its way out. Upstairs in her crib, Dream was hollering in a certain shrill, hysterical way which meant she wasn't calming down anytime soon. Plain Jane came down the stairs more quickly than I'd ever seen her move.

Bunny, Plain Jane said, was not in her room. Nor was she in the bathroom, the parlor, the kitchen . . .

It was Jackie who found Bunny sound asleep in a hammock on a screened-in porch on the north side of the house which no one ever used. Bunny woke up when she sensed that we were staring at her.

"What y'all lookin' at?" she barked. "And what's all that racket? Oh . . . the baby. Forgot where I was for a moment." She stretched. "Nice hammock," she said to Mrs. Bailey White, who collapsed into an ancient wicker chair.

"Oh, I see," Bunny said, dragging herself out of the hammock. "Y'all thought I ran off. Thought I let you down, huh." I heard a twinge of resentment in her voice.

"Well, we didn't know what to think," said

ABOUT THE AUTHOR

Amy Hill Hearth is the author of *Miss Dreamsville and the Collier County Women's Literary Society,* in addition to author or coauthor of seven nonfiction books, including *Having Our Say: The Delany Sisters' First 100 Years,* the *New York Times* bestseller-turned-Broadway-play. Hearth, a former writer for *The New York Times,* began her career as a reporter at a small daily newspaper in Florida, where she met her future husband, Blair (a Collier County native). She is a graduate of the University of Tampa.

The employees of Thorndike Press hope you have enjoyed this Large Print book. All our Thorndike, Wheeler, and Kennebec Large Print titles are designed for easy reading, and all our books are made to last. Other Thorndike Press Large Print books are available at your library, through selected bookstores, or directly from us.

For information about titles, please call:
  (800) 223-1244

or visit our Web site at:
  http://gale.cengage.com/thorndike

To share your comments, please write:
  Publisher
  Thorndike Press
  10 Water St., Suite 310
  Waterville, ME 04901